You Are My Sunshine and Other Stories

This is a work of fiction. All characters, organizations, and events portrayed in this collection are either products of the author's imagination or are reproduced as fiction.

You Are My Sunshine and Other Stories

Cover art by Rachel Lobbenberg
rachelux.myportfolio.com

Edited by Selena Middleton

Published by Stelliform Press
Hamilton, Ontario, Canada
www.stelliform.press

Printed on 100% recycled paper

Library and Archives Canada Cataloguing in Publication
Title: You are my sunshine : and other stories / Octavia Cade.
Names: Cade, Octavia, 1977- author.
Identifiers: Canadiana (print) 20230184758 | Canadiana (ebook) 20230184812 |
ISBN 9781778092640 (softcover) | ISBN 9781778092657 (EPUB)
Classification: LCC PR9639.4.C33 Y68 2023 | DDC 823/.92—dc23

YOU ARE MY SUNSHINE

AND OTHER STORIES

OCTAVIA CADE

Stelliform Press
Hamilton, Ontario

Table of Contents

We Feed the Bears of Fire and Ice....5
Eight Things We Found Under the Ice, After the Arctic Melted....19
You Are My Sunshine....23
Our Flesh was Bred for This....64
Tidemarks....67
Gone to Earth....76
Inside the Body of Relatives....88
Pollen and Salt....99
The Streams are Paved with Fish Traps....109
Resilience....121
Tranquility....129
The Body Politic....141
The Stone Wētā....144
Come Water, Be One of Us....160
Indicator Species....167
You're Not the Only One....170
Metamorphosis....180
The History of a Coral Future....191

We Feed the Bears of Fire and Ice

Look at what we woke.

✹

We feed them lies and watch them burn for it.

Koala bears rarely run during bush fires. Their instinct at danger is to climb up into canopy, where the leaves are shot through with eucalyptus oil, and flammable. They cling to the trunk with charred paws when it begins to burn, the thin bark catching easily and falling off in flaming strips. It sets their fur alight.

They die screaming.

✹

Polar bears need pack ice to hunt. When the ice breaks up they swim until their strength runs out, or pull themselves onto continent and walk until their muscles waste, until they drag their back legs behind them and fur fails to cover their ribs. They're too slow and too starved to find food, and they drag themselves along until they can't anymore.

They die without the strength to scream.

✹

Look at what we woke.

❁

Darwin is now called The City of Fire. Thermal imagery photographs show red streams through the streets, along the exposed surfaces of buildings. These are as hot as 70° C, and we who still live and work in Darwin do so underground. Sewers have been hollowed further, pipes opened up into giant arching chambers beneath the steaming soil, and at each entrance are thick grates, and guarded, because the saltwater crocodiles swim underground as well, with the sewers opening up to the sea and the storm water drains — dusty for most of the year, until hurricane season — letting the smaller ones slip through.

They grow large beneath, as the fires grow large above.

❁

The ground is wetter. It holds the chill less, and bread baskets move north. More of the lands under long sun are opened up for agriculture, farmers moving slowly polewards, for climate has changed the patterns of growing and there are places that once produced that don't anymore, or don't so much, and Canada has water to spare now which is more than can be said for California, re-enacting Steinbeck as its vineyards wither. The further north we move, out of heat and into wilderness, the more susceptible we are to being eaten rather than eating ourselves.

The more we come to think it's deserved. After all, we let it happen.

❁

Scientific American, 8 February 2016: Australia Cuts 110 Climate Scientist Jobs.[1]

❋

Sacrifices have to be made. We didn't do it then, so we have to do it now.

Our ancestors, some of them, tied their heretics to posts and placed kindling around them, lit them up as candles for punishment. Our sacrifice is not religious, but when we fasten a person to their own fire-stake and stack eucalyptus leaves around their feet, leave them wailing through the heat of day until the fire comes for them, the impulse is no different. Propitiation, atonement, mercy.

Sometimes heatstroke renders them insensible before the fire comes. Sometimes we think these are the better days, but sometimes we build our altars in the early morning, set them in places where we can see the sparks already settling, because sacrifice, we think, should be screaming.

❋

Our ancestors, some of them, starved the criminals and the people they claimed as useless, denied them food in times of short resource, let them go out into the wild and the dark to die alone, or to survive as best they could away from community. Now when we leave a person to exposure we take no chances of them coming back. We leave them in the wilderness, strip them naked, slash the tendons in the backs of their legs so that they can only crawl away from the starving bear that their blood calls.

---

1 https://www.scientificamerican.com/article/australia-cuts-110-climate-scientist-jobs/

Most often shock and blood loss leaves them unconscious; they don't feel the claws and the jaws and the tearing. And sometimes the silence is better even, because sacrifice, we think, should not always draw attention to itself with screaming.

❋

Lies have such a monstrous *weight.*

We knew what we were doing. We didn't know what would come of it.

Monsters are too busy lying to think ahead.

❋

The koala comes with burning.

It stalks through the streets, its body the size of skyscrapers, and we've watched it bring those flaming feet down and braced for impact and earthquakes, because something that size should shatter the balance of small-minded things when it moves, but for all fire comes with noise and substance all the conflagration is above ground.

All we do is wrap our heads with wet cloth and crouch beneath, watch the koala as it burns itself out and takes the city with it.

❋

Hunger comes down from the north, an enormous frozen mouth with teeth like icicles. It paces over ice with furry paws, stretches enormous over countryside. We watch as it walks overhead, the hunger bear, and its famine claws leave furrows waist deep in the earth. Its head the size of houses, it breathes starvation and we starve under it, or think we do, for the hunger bear was raised with lies and breathes the same through those sharp and unhappy teeth.

When we feel that breath like wind on our own faces we chain ourselves to fridges, not only for the potential for gorging, but because once we've eaten everything within reach it makes us want to walk north, north, and feed ourselves to what we've starved.

❋

Look at what we woke.
Look at what we *made*.

❋

Ghost bears, giant bears, pacing over landscape. They burn and hunt and eat, their paws and eucalyptus breath, their scars and starving claws.

We blister under them. We bleed and freeze. They take no notice. We're so small, compared to them, to the blizzards and fire storms of their bodies. No wonder they see us as nothing but fuel.

We feed them pieces of ourselves. Sacrificial offerings, to make them go away.

Sometimes it even works.

❋

The stake, the bones and flesh and screaming, are always burned to ash. These blow away in scalding winds, the ground baked so hard that it's hard for us to dig the next hole, to set the next post. It's a filthy job and an unhappy one, but we do it because the circle of blackened earth around the post is large, but often limited. More often than not, once the red bear eats it blows itself out, doesn't drag that massive body through the rest of Darwin, doesn't burn what remains of city and fields and food stores, the fishing docks down at the harbor.

One of us burns, or we all do.

❋

The jaws of the hunger bear bite through bone as though it is a soft and spongy thing. We hear it eat, out on the remains of ice, though the exposed, the ones with their tendons cut, are little more than mouthfuls. But sacrifice never meant satiation, which is all to the good as there's nothing that could fill up the hunger bear anyway, and if we didn't keep it away with blood-offering it would loom over all our cities, would bring its great paw down on houses and schools and shops until we all ran out, swarmed out of our little places like termites, knowing that it meant being devoured but the emptiness in our guts a promise that devouring is the quicker option, the kinder death.

One of us feeds, or we all do. Every day we feed, because every day we lied.

❋

Science, 25 August 2017: DOE Denies It has Policy to Remove 'Climate Change' from Agency Materials.[2]
The Scientist, 29 August 2017: Researchers Advised to Remove Climate Change Language.[3]

❋

2 http://www.sciencemag.org/news/2017/08/doe-denies-it-has-policy-remove-climate-change-agency-materials

3 https://www.the-scientist.com/?articles.view/articleNo/50220/title/Researchers-Advised-to-Remove-Climate-Change-Language/

Every day we lied, and every day we used truth to do it:

Bears have died for climate before. The giant koala, *Phascolarctos stirtoni,* is a Pleistocene relative of today's koala. Its common name is relative, for the giant koala was only a third again as large as its modern kin, not near as large as the holocaust in koala shape that stalks our cities, but size didn't save it in the end. It is hypothesized that the giant koala died because the climate changed, because of the effect that change had on sources of nutrition.

(Today, increased atmospheric carbon dioxide reduces the nutrients available in eucalyptus leaves, increases the amount of toxic tannins. There's starvation here as well, and poison to go with burning, the dehydration deaths caused by leaves with too little water.)

Bears have lived for climate before. Late in the Pleistocene, a population of brown bears, *Ursus arctos,* adapted to the ecology of their polar home. They began to eat a diet that was primarily meat, primarily marine, and their ability to process large amounts of animal fat without cardio-pulmonary consequence developed, differentiating them from their brown cousins. Their fur lightened, their molars changed. A new species, and an iconic one, bred on the border lines of ice age.

(Today, increasing temperatures lead to loss of ice and the polar bears are moving inland, into brown bear territory. The two interbreed, producing fertile offspring and suggesting that genetic change has not yet reached true species-level difference.)

This is how it goes: Climate change is a hack, a fraud, a politically motivated recipe for economic failure. It's happened in the past, without us, for billions of years the climate changed without us. We can't affect the climate, we're only one species and the world is so large and so complex, and besides God would never allow it.

It's bad science. It's hippie emotionalism. Species come and go, and humans are the only important one anyway. Organisms that can't adapt to changing conditions should just die. It's sad, but it's not our fault.

Photographs of koalas with burned paws are shared around the world. We watch them being given water from a fireman's drink bottle, watch them face down on a veterinary table with each paw soaking in little tubs, wearing colorful protective wee mittens over bandages and burned flesh, and donations of those home-made mittens are sent from far-off countries. Hundreds of mittens, thousands of them, and it's an easy way for us to put off responsibility, pretending that helping in small ways makes up for refusing the large ones.

(The small helps are necessary too.)

The starving bears tug heartstrings. There's a guilt that's hard to look at, so when they take someone who's wandered too close, the waves of meat moving north, we look away and try not to blame. It's easier to refuse responsibility when the refusal's on both sides, and the bears never take a lot.

There's not enough of them left to make a dent, in any case.

(Forgiveness can sometimes be stronger than fear.)

If we don't look, everything is normal. If we don't look, it's not happening.

❋

Scientific American, 31 October 2017: Government Scientist Blocked from Talking About Climate and Wildfires.[4]

❋

The ecology of Australia is adapted to fire. Its evolution is one of burning. The eucalypts, especially, are serotinous. The seeds survive bushfires in woody casings that open after flames. The leaves take a long time to break down and are impregnated with flammable oils; the bark shreds off in thin pieces. Alight, they can be blown over distance.

One lit match, and the fire will spread and spread.

(Organisms that can't adapt to changing conditions should just die.)

We have adapted to fire.

We volunteer for burning, when the crocodiles have taken our families, when the fire has taken our features. Our world is one of sunlight anyway, of pain and burning and it is the world of our creation, the world which our lies have made. When the fire koala breathes on us, hot gusts in our faces set our hair alight, set our lungs to scalding and the screaming stops then, our hands still tugging futile at the stake they've been tied to and we die in sizzling clouds of eucalyptus oil with the claws and burning fur of the koala brushing up against us.

All our extremes were *normal*, they said.

---

[4] https://www.scientificamerican.com/article/government-scientist-blocked-from-talking-about-climate-and-wildfires/

❁

The ecology of the Arctic is adapted to ice. Its evolution is one of dry freezing: permafrost, glaciers, sea ice, the frigid oceanic currents. Bearded seals are a favorite food of polar bears. The seals are able to survive the cold primarily due to their thick layers of blubber, a highly calorific fat content that makes them valuable prey for marine carnivores. The increasing temperatures and subsequent reduction in ice means that the bearded seals are harder to stalk, and harder to catch.

Organisms that can't adapt to changing conditions should just die, they said.

We have adapted to ice loss.

We volunteer for exposure when the hunger grows too great, when our children have opened up their bellies with scalpels to pack the food in deeper, when their blood on our hands has a meaty, delicious flavor. When the hunger bear stands over us, body big enough to block out the sun and its ribs poking through the horror-structure of its body, the screams are frozen in our lungs, full of icicles now and longing. The last thing we smell is our bellies, opened up and steaming, the enticement of blood and our own fingers tearing at bowels, the nails not long enough to really join in the feasting.

Catastrophic extremes are only to be expected, they said.

❁

The bears, the bears.

We feed the bears of fire and ice, we feed them lies, we feed them twice.

We lied and woke them up.

❁

Heatstroke takes more lives than invasion. Underground is cooler, but we can't stay there forever and even those south of us are burning in their cities. There's transport, supplies come in from other places, the remains of growing things for food. It's easier at night when the heat gnaws less at bones but crocodiles are night hunters and they're growing larger, and there's not enough night vision goggles to keep their silent, heavy tread away.

It's safer in sunlight, barely, but the heatstroke bites with red teeth, more dangerous than mouths.

Hunger takes more lives than invasion. For all the landscape's changing, the wild places getting smaller and crowding the animals into our back yards, making them walk our streets, it doesn't stop us eating. That's the life instinct: to go on, to consume, and some of us don't have enough and die of it, while some of us have more than enough and it's still not, because the long snout of hunger lies beneath and ready to ambush. It wakes us in the night and sets us to stuffing, makes us burst our own bellies with the lies we fed ourselves, makes us walk out into dark streets where the wolves scavenge, where the brown bears lie in wait.

It's safer in sunlight, but who wants to spend all their life with clear vision anyway. Our vision is already clear enough.

We came for them first, the ones who lied the best.

We had to. Every organism adapts to their environment; it was a matter of survival. Sacrifice means the holocaust above dies down at night. Even the buildings cool, the tar settles in the streets and come early morning we can walk across it without sticking, while the crocodile tracks and the great marks of the fire bear as it drags its claws through the city stand rigid around us before the roads melt again into straightness. The fire bear always comes back during the day. It stays away longer if we give it something new to consume ... something not eucalypt because we raised the fire bear on lies and that's what it likes best to eat.

It dies down in winter, the hunger storm without, the frozen winds. The ice that's left reforms, the polar bears that are left scramble to the floes for hunting, but the summer always comes back with starvation and they have to come for us instead. And we had to come for them — for the ones who lied the best, because if we lie as slick as seals the lies seep out of us like so much oily blubber, give a shiny bursting gloss to skin. The more the hunger bear eats of lies, the longer the winters last.

This makes us careful about our lies, doling them out in small proportion when once we spewed and swallowed them like the smell of eucalyptus leaves, like the soft giving flesh of fat and fish.

❋

The Guardian, 26 May 2016: Australia Scrubbed from UN Climate Change Report after Government Intervention.[5]

❋

I'm a liar too. A koala is a marsupial, not a bear.

Tourist dollars, industry profits, narrative structure. Whatever it's for, we lie to make a point.

❋

[5] https://www.theguardian.com/environment/2016/may/27/australia-scrubbed-from-un-climate-change-report-after-government-intervention

Those of us who know we are liars, well. We begin to think of justice, because if ever there is an ideal constructed out of falsity it is that, and we are all familiar.

Justice becomes a temptation, and a cause.

We set fire to them first, the worst of the liars. When the city started burning down, when it was too hot to live above ground and those monstrous footprints started burning city blocks we dragged out the politicians who'd signed and bribed and looked away, strung them from lamp-posts with their guts cut out and hanging down, set fire to their entrails while they were still living because the screaming brought the bear from the suburbs, from the supermarkets, from trying to force its face through grating into the drains where we huddled, the iron glowing and bending sticky-soft around that searching face.

We took knives to them first, the polluters and the lobbyists, the ones that we let look away for profit, the ones whose money we took to look away in turn, but money didn't do much for us when the hunger bear came and it didn't do much for them either, didn't patch together their tendons with bank notes as the bear stalked them bloody, didn't let them call for help because we stuffed their gullets before we cut them, pouched their cheeks with promissory notes the color of bribes and lies, the ones that said they could buy anything, including bears.

But bears cannot be bought. Which is why, when we look at them, we see the mirrors in their starved and burning eyes, the ones that say we let it happen, we let our greed and their greed call the bears and now they've come and we've nothing left but sacrifice.

Hot breath against cheek. *Was it worth it,* says the koala, its body the size of skyscrapers.

Cold claw against stomach. *How do your lies taste now,* says the polar bear, its head the size of houses.

✹

They taste like ice and ashes. They taste like the breath of the bear that ate our homework. The payment's in the post the email never came it was fire-based ecology anyway we don't feel well not all scientists agree a bear ate our grandmother died after eating homework glaciers have always come and gone the car wouldn't start there's an accident on the roads danger to the economy we'll be right there with the money homework promises these extremes are normal ate our homework it would have happened anyway five minutes we'll be there in *five minutes* of course we didn't mean it like that one person can't do anything one species better you than us better them than us it'll be over soon…

This is how it goes.

✹

Look at what we woke.
Look at what we woke *in us*.

✹

There's a lot less liars now.

Eight Things We Found Under the Ice, After the Arctic Melted

Mammoth bones, mammoth flesh. Hair still attached to skin and streaming down, softening from ice into strands. Tusks to be traded, baby mammoths given names and wrapped up in glass in museums, little lost calves brought in from the cold. Skins scrapings to be smeared over microscope slides. It's a good thing they're all so very dead, else it'd be called vivisection. Now they're just opportunity, because it's one thing to let the dead rest but when they've been dead so very, very long, we figure they'll stop minding.

It is, after all, opportunity. There's all that oil, under the surface, and the access to it is so much easier now. It's not just the mammoths. Dead plants, dead forests, all broken down into resurrection parts, life brought back in form of energy because energy transforms and that's how we go from life to lifestyle: the application of energy to inertia, the disinclination for sacrifice. The mammoths are already dead, stopping climate change won't bring them back, and we don't have the same fascination for their descendants.

The third thing dug up from under the ice is irony, because elephants remain a popular creature, an icon of conservation, but they don't live in the Arctic so we pop the irony back in a box and bury it again because some visibilities are too many and we've only got two eyes, one for forward and one for backward so the present garners much less attention. Besides, there's opportunity under ice and if we were *very* clever, we would approach the oil companies of the world and ask for donations to bring the mammoths back. Science is expensive, and if there are enough mammoths, herds and herds of them, then their grazing will transform vegetation, bring back the grasslands and alter albedo and that will help get the temperature back down, it's a win for everyone.

The fourth thing is teeth, and they're only under a very thin layer, we should have found them first but we weren't looking that hard, really, it was mostly kids sifting through that damp and melting rubble that came up with the things. The mouths they're from are, unlike the mammoths, barely dead. Polar bears without pack ice, starving on coasts and coming south. Brown bears moving north into warming continents. The polar bears and the brown bears interbreeding to make more bears: bears with the physical characteristics of both parents but the behavioral attributes of *Ursus maritimus*, the hyper-carnivore, which has always looked on us as a food source. (Brown, lie down. White, goodnight.) The first teeth found are weakened from hunger, but the more teeth are found the more we find that warm human irony is a substitute for seal flesh and we didn't bury that deep enough bears couldn't dig it up.

Which begs the fifth thing we found in the ice: a wistful, oily sort of hope, slicked up so we could swallow down, because the mammoths look like elephants and we remember the elephants enough for associations to spill over, a little, when that spillage isn't so costly to us. Regardless of actual temperament, we tend to think of elephants in terms of dignity and mourning, but there's nothing says a mammoth has to mature the same way. For all we know the fucking things will have the temperaments of buffalo and stomp around those hoped-for grasslands looking for other things to trample. May they find them at oil fields. Herds of mammoth, bearing down, blood on their tusks. Hybrid bears, blood on their teeth. Monstrous, perhaps, far removed from those bare little beasts behind museum glass, those starving creatures without ice, but potentially worth it.

Still, we don't live in a horror film. There are few times I say that with rue but the prospect of a herd of pissed-off mammoths is frankly sympathetic. Which is where number six comes in. You wouldn't think shame could be unearthed from a melting ecosystem but there it is — like the teeth, like the oil, she's not buried deep enough. Shame, it turns out, was buried with all those documents on the future of climate. I'd blame Big Oil and it's true their nasty fingerprints are all over it, and certainly no one ever accused any of them of even a passing association with conscience (how could they, when she was buried so far away?) but misinformation and the censorship of data is too vast a conspiracy for the rest of us not to have a hand in it. Not everyone's a scientist, excising what they can't explain away. Not everyone's an executive, hauling in ridiculous money to doom their descendants. We're just the ones letting them get away with it, and so when shame asks for a very large saddle and a necklace of bear teeth and says she wants to travel north to look for viruses, well. It's hard not to look her in the face and wonder how horror and sympathy have come to be so damn entwined.

Seven is buried in the ice, tucked away like smallpox in a lab. Those Arctic microbes, locked in the soil beneath all that frozen water, except when the ice goes and the temperature rises and the microbes wake up, well. Who's surprised? We're in the resurrection business now. (Resurrection's so much more exciting than change in consumerism, it's science to the rescue so we don't have to stomach self-control.) Somewhere, shame is cackling her head off and hoping that half of us act like unexpected mammoths, irrational in our behavior in the face of disease. I suspect that, even buried deep as she was, she saw the headlines. Then again, nature *is* a balance. If we're going to dig up the dead so cavalierly we should get used to burying more of them as well.

That's the eighth thing we found when the ice melted: scribbled on the back of shareholder receipts, the reminder to go buy a fucking shovel.

You Are My Sunshine

The first one he found had been left in his letterbox. It hadn't been wrapped in any way; it certainly hadn't been delivered by the postman, who was retching on Cyrus' porch. It had been stuffed in, just as it was. A severed arm, a *human* arm, and with a handwritten note carefully tied with baling twine about the wrist.

I'm sorry.

Cyrus didn't know who the apology was for, but he thought it should probably have been for the postman. "I opened the box to put your mail in and it was *right there,*" he said. The letterbox was big, because Cyrus often received parcels from his mother, parcels full of fruitcake and other supposed treats which he didn't much like and never ate, but always pretended gratitude for because she was his mother and doing her best to show love and he loved her in return. Even so, the size of the letterbox wasn't enough to easily accommodate the arm. Folded in on itself, hinged at the elbow, it had still been wedged in. Gingerly, Cyrus reached out to touch before thinking better of it. For a brief moment he thought he might have been the victim of a practical joke, one of the local kids trying to scare him with a rubber limb, but the flesh was clammy and tacky with half-dried blood, and the smell of it — still faint, but with a sour pork smell that would draw flies sooner rather than later — disabused him of the notion.

"I swear to God it wasn't there yesterday," said the postman. "I didn't put it there, it's not mine!"

The postman still had both his arms, so that wasn't exactly news, but Cyrus could understand the need for disclaimers. He did it himself when the police came. The subsequent interview was prolonged incomprehension. No, he had no idea who would do this. No, he didn't have any enemies. No, he hadn't seen anyone come to the gate that morning — he'd been on the other side of the house, working on notes for a talk he was due to give on the effects of wasting disease on local sea star populations.

"You work at the aquarium?" said the cop, and Cyrus nodded.

"Marine biologist," he said.

"I don't suppose you see a lot of dismemberment up there," said cop.

"You'd be surprised," said Cyrus.

❋

Cyrus had grown up inland, surrounded by sunflowers. He always knew he wouldn't stay in the place of his birth, but when he left for the coast, for the ocean that had called to him since he was small, he took the sunflowers with him. A handful of seeds, and he planted them wherever he went. When he settled, at last, in the house he planned to stay in forever, or for as long as the rising tides let him stay, he circled the fields around his little rural house with sunflowers, with bright, leggy bursts of them, and felt at home.

He didn't raise them for seeds, like his parents did, or for oil. He raised them as a reminder of the dead. As a reminder of *Pycnopodia helianthoides*, the sunflower sea star, the largest of the Pacific starfish. The largest of all the starfish, excepting only a little-seen creature, a spindly gargantuan beast that lurked in the deep oceans of the Gulf of Mexico. Cyrus had loved the sunflower sea star ever since he'd seen a picture of them as a boy, bright and leggy and larger across than he could spread his small arms.

When they were young, the sunflowers outside his bedroom window oriented themselves towards the sun, and Cyrus, when he had been young himself, hoped for a similar heliotropism with the sea stars. He'd dreamed that he was underwater, diving with a bright torch, and the sea stars turned to him as he swam, waving their arms as if to say hello. He'd known the dreams weren't real, but he'd wanted them to be. For a year, the only crayons he'd used had been blue and yellow, sea stars in water, long arms with petals attached. Eventually he ran out of yellow and started using oranges and purples too, because the sunflower sea stars he loved were not a perfect reflection of the sunflowers he lived with. Their colors were broader, but Cyrus didn't care. He loved the sea stars, and he came to love the flowers because of the sea stars, and as an adult his sense-memories of both were shot through with the scent of wax, the slippery-soap feeling of crayons in his fingers.

The wax, at least, was malleable. If he left the crayons out in sunshine (by the beach, in the fields) they would soften in the heat and he could shape them, stretch them out, pinch them at the ends, turn the instruments of his design into little reaching arms, and stud them with sunflower seeds for texture. They didn't look like sea star arms, not really, but he didn't know then that such shapes were malleable, too.

When he did know, when the monstrous consequence of wasting had crawled out of oceans and disintegrated on shores, washed up in shaking, amorphous shapes of putrefying jelly, it was not the only mortification he had come to observe. It was certainly not the only remnants of flesh he had come to accept.

The sea star wasting disease was linked to warming waters. Other than that, the causes were murky, and still being researched. Cyrus was one of the researchers. He hadn't made it to the ocean, dropping sunflower seeds behind him, just to see that ocean emptied when the sunflower sea star, and all the other sea stars, disintegrated into the undead.

The other name of this disease was zombie starfish. More attention-getting than wasting disease, which sounded like consumption. Ironically, one of the first signs was the lack thereof — affected sea stars lost their appetite, moped about on the ocean floor, listless and starving. Only then did they start to fall apart. Their limbs lost their grip, twisted and shriveled and fell off. Then those dismembered limbs *kept moving,* the body melting and rotting while still alive. The limbs died too, soon after, but for a time they were the living dead, the remnants of an organism which, in their multitudes, were so reminiscent of fields of sunflowers scattered over a sea floor. That sea floor was to Cyrus, with his pockets full of seeds, a place where the sea stars were increasingly not.

Where *all* the sea stars were increasingly not.

Desperation drove Cyrus to unthinkable solutions.

"They're not solutions," said Marjorie. He had never met her in person; she was a biologist working down on the Great Barrier Reef, or what remained of it. Those remains weren't much: bleached skeletons and empty spaces where once there had been an ecosystem that could be seen from space. He'd contacted her, contacted everyone in the field, trying to brainstorm a stopgap to annihilation. Translocation of surviving organisms — the attempt to introduce a population into other waters — was likely a foolish endeavor, but he would have done anything to keep the sunflower sea stars alive.

"They're dying," he said. "I can't help them. I don't know what's causing it. I only know if we don't do something there'll be no sea stars in the North Pacific anymore. None. Their populations are in freefall. They're *disintegrating* in the water."

"Good," said Marjorie. "Fucking things. I hope they die, and the sooner the better."

It was the most emotion Cyrus had ever seen from her. He wasn't sure which of them signed off first, but he was sure he was too disgusted to speak with her again.

The message came a few days later, text only.

I'm sorry.

It took him a long time to answer. He wasn't sure if he should, if it was worth asking. Some knowledge could never be anything but hurtful. But there were sunflowers outside, and an old scent of wax on his fingers, and he had learned to see similarities, to make connections, when he could.

"Why do you hate them?" he wondered. Part of him hadn't expected her to answer, but the video call went through and he could see her, wild-haired, with dark circles under her eyes and emptiness in her gaze.

Marjorie shared her screen, showing him photographs of the wastelands where the Reef had been. Some of those pictures were of sea stars. *Acanthaster planci*, the crown-of-thorns starfish. "They feed on coral," she said. "When the waters warmed, the starfish came. They migrated south into the Reef, great hungry waves of them. They ate *everything*. Everything in their path. Oh, it was us too. We ate the Reef as much as they did. I think I hate them because those bloody starfish *are* us. Neither of us cared about anything but consumption, about more and more, and we ate the Reef together, and now there's nothing left. The waters warmed, and the starfish swarmed, and they took everything."

He could hear the sorrow in her voice. He wasn't immune. The death of the Great Barrier Reef had been a blow for biologists everywhere; he had thought himself lucky that at least he had sea stars left to love.

He hoped Marjorie had something left to love, that she had something to anchor her psyche enough that sorrow expressed itself in ways other than Grief.

"Do you know," she asked him, "how we tried to kill them? At first it was with machetes. We hacked them apart, one at a time. But there were so many, and they were so meaty, and it took so long. We could never hack enough. Do you know how hard it is to swing a machete underwater? It was almost easier to drag the starfish to the surface and hack them to death there. But then we found another way. A quicker way — just a bit of vinegar. We'd inject them with vinegar, dozens at a time, *hundreds* at a time. They'd dissolve from the inside-out.

"I bet you think that's cruel, don't you?" she said.

Cyrus did think that. All the time he'd spent trying to keep his sunflowers from disintegrating, from spreading their beautiful bodies across the floor of the ocean ... and he'd wanted to send them to a place where conservationists had brought disintegration to sea stars of their own accord.

"I have thought very much less about whether it is cruel than I have about whether it is necessary," said Marjorie. "We were so very, very desperate."

"It doesn't sound like it was enough," said Cyrus.

"It wasn't." A blunt assessment, and the severity of it was underlined by the way her fingers twisted in the rough hem of her shirt. The edges had begun to fray — Cyrus could see the threads caught up in her fingers — and he wondered if she knew she was shredding the fabric, or if the destruction was purely unconscious.

"I guess it's my turn to be sorry." Her sorrow grieved him, borne as it was from the death of starfish.

Marjorie sniffed at him. "What good is your sorrow to me?" she said, and logged off before he could answer.

When, weeks later, Cyrus heard she had left employment at the university, a victim of the Grief, he was not exactly surprised. The Grief spread through communities like a tsunami, a looming, terrible series of waves that undercut sanity. He wasn't a psychologist, or a medical doctor. He couldn't explain why some people fell into suicidal depression at the ecological loss around them, but then he didn't know if he needed to explain it. He had neither the words nor the desire … only a small, hopeless suspicion that the waves were coming ever nearer his own feet, as the sea stars he loved died so terribly around him, and then reanimated in their dismembered parts before dying again.

His mother sent him fruitcakes. They were steeped in brandy, and studded with almonds and horrid, violently colored cherries that tasted of chemicals and sadness. They would probably survive the end of the world, her fruitcakes, and that was likely why she sent them. As a reminder that some things could survive, and that she expected him to be one of them. It couldn't have been easy to have a son so utterly in love with things that were dying, not in an age of Grief, but his mother wasn't a biologist. She wasn't a scientist. She was a farmer's wife who worked part-time in a hardware store and he didn't know how to tell her how afraid he was of his own ineffectiveness. She'd try to feed him, tell him to buck up and make the best of it. Even her cakes were given to practicality.

He should have made more of an effort to eat them, but he found them too heavy to be appetizing. Too many things were already pressing on him; his mother's love was just another burden to carry.

The severed arm was almost an excuse for fruitcake. The cake was nearly the only alcohol in the house, bar the bottle of rubbing alcohol he kept in the bathroom in case of emergencies. If he started drinking, there was a chance he wouldn't stop, but any alcohol in the fruitcake was surely cooked off. It would be a placebo more than anything else, but if a severed limb stuffed in a letterbox didn't call for at least a placebo then Cyrus didn't know what did.

The postman refused a piece of cake. "I never want to eat again," he said. "Have you considered getting a PO Box in town?"

"I'm not using this one again, that's for sure," said Cyrus. The police were taking it away for evidence. "If they left it here, I'd probably burn it," he said.

"I'd lend you the matches," said the postman. His name was Jerry, and when he'd wobbled off to deliver the rest of his round, Cyrus thought he'd seen the last of him, but that evening Jerry was back. There was a crate of beer strapped to the back of his bike.

"Fuck this for a bunch of hammers," he said. "I don't know what that means, exactly, but it was all I could think today, after ..." One hand, the hand not holding a beer, waved toward where the mailbox had been. "I was working as an accountant, you know? Long hours, hunched over a computer, bashing my brains out over other people's dodgy tax returns. I got so sick of it, thought I'd pack it in and get a job in the fresh air. Turns out fresh air smells like a serial killer's letterbox."

"There's so many things wrong with that I don't know where to start," said Cyrus. He'd decided to forgo teetotalism for the day, on the grounds that being drunk could only improve things. "First, you don't know a serial killer did that. Second, if they did, it could be me and what're *you* doing, bringing beer to a serial killer?"

"Please." Jerry rolled his eyes in an exaggerated way that made Cyrus wonder how many beers ahead he was. "You looked sicker than I did. And I stopped to be sick twice, and one of those times was in someone's prize azaleas and the other was in a birdbath, so when I say you looked worse, you can believe it. Besides, who else but a serial killer would stuff an arm in a letterbox? That's logic irrefutable, that is."

Cyrus tried to refute it, but couldn't. "If I were you I'd be worrying about the rest of the body and the rest of the letterboxes," he said. "Are you going to be finding pieces for days, do you reckon? Got any special-sized parcels lately?"

Jerry shot him a jaundiced glance. "You're a terrible person. I can see why some bastard sent you an arm."

It was not, unfortunately, the only arm.

Cyrus hadn't asked after the owner of the first arm. He hadn't wanted to know. There was a victim out there, someone who had been hurt and mutilated and left in pieces for strangers to find, and he thought they deserved better than a morbid curiosity that would help neither them nor him. He did his best to carry on and not think about it, and found it less difficult than he anticipated.

Then the second arm turned up, and it was harder to ignore. Firstly because it had been left on his porch, placed carefully on the doormat where he couldn't help but see it when he stepped out the door, and secondly, because the arm belonged to a woman. It was delicate, light-boned, and the nails were freshly manicured. There was one letter on each nail, and together they spelled out *SORRY*.

What good is your sorrow to me? Marjorie had asked him that, so entirely convinced of the ineptitude of any possible answer that she hadn't bothered to stay on the call. At the time it had felt like an attack. Now the absolute dismissal in her voice echoed in his head. Some sins were so enormous that apologies were worthless.

The arm that had been severed and stuffed into his letterbox had been so crammed in there that he hadn't been able to make out any particular characteristics. The *I'm sorry* tag had been facing the front of the letterbox, making it hard to miss, but Cyrus hadn't looked for a single second longer than he'd had to before calling the police. He didn't even know whether the arm belonged to a man or a woman. The only thing he was sure of was that it was too large to belong to a child. He was grateful for that.

The second arm, the arm on his doorstep, had personality.

The third arm had its useless apology tattooed along the forearm. It had been left in one of his fields, with sunflowers growing up around it. The fourth had a sunflower painted on the palm of its hand. The fifth was strung up from a dozen sunflowers, attached to their stems with yellow ribbons to take the weight, hovering three feet above the ground. The sixth he found nailed palm-up along the top of his front fence. There were sunflower seeds in the palm; birds were perched on dead fingers and pecking.

All of the arms were from different people. Sometimes there was a week between appearances. Sometimes it was only a day. One morning, after another fruitless conversation with police, he walked the sunflowers fields around his little house and found four planted amidst the sunflowers with their fingers reaching for heaven, painted green and gold. All of them had apologies written somewhere on their flesh.

It could only be Grief, he thought. It could only, could only, could only be Grief.

"If I were you'd I'd move," said Jerry. "Just pack up, find somewhere else to live. Someplace where you can go outside and not trip over bits of corpses."

This would have been the sensible solution. If he hadn't lived alone Cyrus might have considered it, but he had no one to protect but himself. Besides, the apologies that came with the dead flesh made him think that someone was looking for his forgiveness — and anyone unbalanced enough, or obsessed enough, to plant arms in fields of sunflowers would surely follow him if he left. At least at home he was on familiar ground.

That was what he told Jerry, anyway, and his mother, and his colleagues at the aquarium, who were beginning to look at him with a careful distance that was not quite suspicion but which was at least an acknowledgment of difference. As if he were beginning to drift to the outside of the herd, where the predators were.

The truth was he couldn't bring himself to leave the sunflowers. It would have been abandonment. He'd left them before, taken seeds from the farm he grew up on and made a place for them on the coast. Rationality said that he'd prompted nothing by doing so, made no provocation. Rationality said that he had no influence over the wasting disease, but he'd left the sunflowers once before, and now the sea stars who had their name were leaving him, and if he left again in return it would be nothing but the continuation of a cycle, an increasing current of feedback through ever darker and emptier waters.

Ridiculous to be so superstitious, but once he'd admitted to himself the truth of his desire to stay, he couldn't make himself believe the superstition was wrong.

If anyone had ever told Cyrus he could get used to the appearance of severed limbs in his garden, he would have thought them a liar, or insane — but he did get used to them.

"There's something fucked up with you," said Jerry. "Maybe you should think about, you know, seeing someone."

"It's not Grief," said Cyrus.

"How do you know?"

There was no answer he could give that would adequately explain his certainty. Then again, if it *was* Grief, surely any reasoning, no matter how poor, would make sense in his own mind. That was the way of Grief: a determined undermining of perspective, one that turned solid sanity to salt water and suicide.

He used salt water to fill the birdbath Jerry had brought him. "I live in an apartment," Jerry said. "It's no good to me." The birdbath was the one he had vomited in after he and Cyrus had found the arm in the letterbox. "I kind of felt bad about that," he said.

"They could have just washed it out."

"Yeah, but I bought them a new one anyway. Then I was stuck with the old one, and I thought you've got a garden, you can have it."

"So I can throw up in it myself?"

"You never know," said Jerry. "If those things keep turning up, you might be grateful."

Together, they wrestled the birdbath into place, onto a patch of lawn Cyrus could see from the kitchen window. It was, Cyrus thought, a particularly ugly birdbath.

"Maybe plant some flowers. That might improve it."

"Sunflowers would be tall enough to block it out," said Cyrus. "That'd be an improvement."

"Sunflowers can't block out everything," said Jerry. "And why salt water? I don't think the birds will like it."

"I don't know," said Cyrus. He'd brought a bucket of it back from his last dive, sprinkled it in a circle around his house, sprayed the windows and lintels as if the salt would keep him safe, keep the possibility of Grief at a distance, and keep the arms at a distance as well.

There were many things he did not know, and even more he did not say. Jerry might have intimated the prospect of Grief, but if he were really worried there were doctors he could call, psychologists, and there was nothing that said Cyrus wouldn't be sectioned for his own good, taken away from the sunflowers, away from the sea stars. Yet more and more there wasn't space in residential facilities for those stricken with Grief; a recent spate of people burning themselves alive in anguished protest had led to the immediate hospitalization of the more advanced cases. Cyrus had shown no such predilection; it was possible he'd be left with a more minimal supervision, able to stay in his home, but he didn't want to take the chance. Instead, he woke in the cool early mornings and lay in bed, wondering if that day he'd find another arm, and what he could say to it (what he could do with it) if he did. Cyrus thought that there were three possibilities: beauty, creativity, and love.

1: Beauty

He could acknowledge that he found them beautiful. Not the one in the letterbox, perhaps, that had been a crammed and unglamorous thing, although in fairness he had hardly stopped to examine its aesthetics. For all Cyrus knew, if he had reached in to unfold it, to bring it out into sunlight, there might have been something there to reward him for not looking away. Too late now, the opportunity was gone, but the rest … there'd been something terribly lovely about the painted palm, about the birds who came down for feeding. A generosity, perhaps, and one that survived dismemberment. The yellow ribbons in the field, the carefully painted nails. Cyrus had never painted his own nails. The day after he found the second arm he'd gone to the supermarket — ignoring the burn marks on the pavement outside the door — and bought some nail polish. He'd never looked at that section of the aisle before. There were so many colors to choose from. Not just the pinks and reds that he expected, but brighter colors too. Happier colors.

"Which one do you like?" asked a woman standing next to him. She had dark circles under her eyes and unhappy lines on her face. Her own nails were bare and chipped. She didn't look like she used nail polish any more than he did.

"All of them," he said. It was true. He could have seen any of these colors underwater, once.

"I don't know if I should be getting any at all," she said. "I've been standing here for half an hour trying to decide. It's not for me. I've a friend who likes to wear it. But she's … she's lost an arm recently."

The colors were suddenly too bright.

"She's been sick for a long time. It wasn't unexpected." Cyrus missed the next few sentences, his hearing dulled as the colors faded. It was a terrible coincidence, that was all. She couldn't have known that an arm had been placed at his door like an offering, that one had been shoved into his letterbox. There was still sickness in the world that had nothing to do with sunflowers, still cancer and diabetes and infection, other reasons for limb loss. "She asked me to pick her up some nail polish," the woman continued. "I think that's brave, don't you? When she can't even put it on herself anymore."

"She could paint her toenails," said Cyrus. "She'd only need one hand for that." It seemed a facile suggestion, but the woman beamed at him, a surprised smile, as if she'd forgotten how and had astonished herself by remembering.

"She could! And I suppose she could paint other parts of her as well, if she wanted. Or she could paint me, after I paint her."

"Then maybe the question is what color do *you* like," said Cyrus.

The woman paused, considering. "I like the yellow," she said. "It's cheerful. Maybe you should get it too. You look like you need cheering up."

He bought the yellow. He bought as well the acetone that would remove it, and he went home and painted and painted, removing the coats of polish that were uneven due to his lack of practice, that slopped over the edges of nails and stained his flesh. When he was done, when his fingers were topped with sunflower yellow and he was happy to look at them, he'd gone walking the fields around his house but it had all been for nothing, because the third arm, the one with the tattoo on it, hadn't arrived yet. There was nothing for him to show his nails to but the sunflowers, and it was all the same to them.

He took the polish off before he went back to work. Some things, he thought, should be private. He painted his toenails instead, the same sunflower yellow, because he could wear that beneath his shoes, beneath his socks, and no one would see or judge him for it. It made him feel as if he were walking on flowers. It made him feel closer, somehow, to the sunflower sea stars in the aquarium tanks. There weren't many of them, and they were kept in quarantine to prevent their developing any symptoms of wasting sickness. The sea stars weren't pets, and Cyrus wouldn't dive down into the tanks to stroke them, but he wanted to. He wanted to tell them they were beautiful and alive and that his feet were tipped with sunflowers. That they were, somehow, the same.

He could imagine what Marjorie would have said to him, if she'd known his thoughts: "If by 'the same' you mean you're both on the verge of falling apart, then yes, I suppose you are."

He rather suspected she'd think that was a good thing. That she'd enjoy his fragmentation, as payment for a loyalty to sea stars that she could no longer fathom herself, linked as they were in her mind to a profound, and very human, destructiveness.

He didn't feel like he was falling apart. He felt as if there should be seeds in his nail beds, as if he should be emptying seed heads and wedging them beneath sunflower nails, but that would be wasteful, and possibly uncomfortable. Instead, he went back to the shop where he'd bought the nail polish and bought all the yellow polish they had, the brightest shade, and used the thin little brushes to paint the soles of his feet, because he remembered the woman in the store saying the polish could be used for more than nails. That calmed him until the fourth arm, the one with the sunflower painted on the palm of its hand. He'd squatted above it when he found it, observing. The paint was beautiful. He wondered if it would wear off. The paint on his feet was wearing off. It flaked in places, and faded in others. The sunflower on the palm of this severed arm would also flake and fade, perhaps. It was possible some would be scraped off, deliberately, during the postmortem examination, and Cyrus found himself distressed at the thought.

If it had been tattooed on, like the tattoo that had apologized from the skin of the third arm, then nothing could take it away.

He took some time off work, and they were glad to see him go. "I'm not surprised you want time off," said his employer. "Try to relax. None of this is your fault."

It was true he'd never dismembered anyone himself. He'd simply watched dismemberment happen to others: the starfish who wasted almost in front of him, their disintegrating limbs twitching, as if asking for the help he didn't know how to give. As terrible as the severed arms were — as terrible, and as almost-lovely — when Cyrus thought of dismemberment now, his thoughts were still first for the sea stars.

That was complicity, perhaps, of a kind more deep-rooted than that which came with cause and effect. He wondered if he should be the one apologizing.

He spent his leave at a tattoo parlor, with needles in his feet. It hurt like hell, but when it was done his soles were a bright, permanent yellow. One foot had patterns in the yellow reminiscent of petals, and the other had patterns of starfish. For days he tried not to walk on them, to let his feet heal. He sat cross-legged, with his soles exposed, and admired how beautiful they were. How beautiful he was becoming.

When his feet had toughened enough to walk on, Cyrus made his way out into the fields. The fifth arm was there, hung up amidst the sunflowers by ribbons. When he touched it, the flesh was warm under the sun.

It made him think of crayons.

✹

His mother sent another fruitcake. This time Cyrus was actually glad for it. He'd eaten fruitcake almost constantly while his feet were recovering. It was high-density food that required little preparation, sweet and filling. It never went off. There had been three fruitcakes in his kitchen cupboards and he ate his way through all of them.

"Funny," he said, giving thanks over the phone. "You'd think I'd be sick of it. But I'm not."

"You always were a fussy child," said Melissa. "Believe it or not I was glad for that. I found you eating crayons when you were a toddler, you know. Yellow crayons, smeared round your mouth. I didn't know how much you'd swallowed so I had to put my fingers down your throat so you'd throw it up. You screamed the house down, screamed through the sick, and afterwards I think you were so disgusted you turned fussy so I wouldn't have to do it again. I'm glad you've grown out of that."

"Eating crayons, or being fussy?" asked Cyrus, grateful he lived several hours away from her. She couldn't see his feet; if she could, there'd be another fuss and it wouldn't be his.

"Both."

"I've been thinking about taking up drawing again," he said. "I know I wasn't that good at it —"

"Oh, you were hopeless," said his mother. "Hopeless. But that doesn't matter. You don't have to be good at something to enjoy it. And hell, if anyone tells you that you shouldn't draw because you're not good at it, tell them what I told that art teacher of yours when you were a kid. Tell them it's abstract, and they'd be lucky to have it on their fridge."

"I remember every other teacher but that one got fruitcake for Christmas," said Cyrus.

"She was a bitch and didn't deserve it," said his mother, complacent. "It'll do you good to have an outlet. I don't know what I'd do if someone left body parts in my letterbox. How could I show my face, honestly? I hope no one's giving you a hard time about it."

"Of course not," said Cyrus, both because it was the truth and because he didn't want her turning up to defend him, as though he were still eight years old with a sagging papier-mâché model of a starfish dragging from one hand, sobbing over a bad grade. The starfish had ended up glued to the fridge with a special adhesive Melissa had gotten from the hardware store — purchased with her ten percent staff discount — and he had the sudden, irrational image of her, her glue, his fridge, and an arm.

No. Just no.

"Are you sure you don't want to come home?"

He was very sure. "At least you can be certain the bathroom won't get wrecked again." That ragged starfish she'd glued to the fridge had never come off. Two months after it had been fixed there, Cyrus had tried to peel it away, to insert a blunt knife between the papier-mâché and the aluminum of the appliance, but his mother's adhesive had defeated him. The bits he'd been able to saw off were little dismemberments of their own, so he'd made some replacement sea stars, made them on the kitchen table with old newspapers and left them to dry, painted them bright colors and let them dry again. Then he'd filled the bathtub with water and salt and starfish, and they'd been bright and pretty, for a few minutes. He'd let the water out to try and salvage the starfish, but the sloughed-off, gluey paper had clogged the drain. He'd left the tap on, tried to force it through, but had only succeeded in flooding the bathroom with salted bathwater and bits of disintegrated starfish.

"I knew then once you found your way to the sea you'd never come back," said Melissa, fondly. "Not that I begrudged taking you to the aquarium. I just didn't want the house turning into one. You'd have had us all swimming with starfish if you could."

"I would," said Cyrus, because the thought of a world without the sunflower sea stars was anathema to him.

"It's just I worry about you, out there, all alone and with a serial killer hacking off people's limbs and leaving them in your garden," said his mother, undeterred. "It's such a nice garden, too. Are people leaving flowers by your gate? I suppose you can use them for compost."

"I don't think it's a serial killer," said Cyrus, choosing to ignore the practical possibilities of mulch. He didn't want to say that flowers had been left, or that he hadn't bothered to collect them. He'd only have been lectured on not letting things go to waste, and then Melissa would have wondered if he was letting other things go to waste, like fruitcake, and was he sure he didn't want her to come down for a bit to help look after him? "I don't know why I don't think it's a serial killer. Maybe it's that the arms are so apologetic."

"Maybe it's a serial killer with manners," said Melissa. "People aren't one thing or the other, you know."

"I know," said Cyrus. "But I don't feel unsafe, truly. It's just ... weird. And I can cope with weird."

His mother didn't comment, but the next parcel — which he had to collect from the post office because he'd never replaced the letterbox and because the postal service was leery of sending employees back his way — contained more than fruitcake. It also had in it a rather nice set of crayons, and a small note: "People say we grow up and put away childish things. I say they should get bent. Have fun, darling. Love, mum. P.S., your dad says hello and he thinks you taking up art again is a good idea. He says it's an armless hobby. I told him you wouldn't appreciate that but he said to tell you anyway."

Cyrus ate the damn cake.

2: Creativity

The crayons sat on his kitchen table, unused, until he went back to work. His colleagues congratulated him on his appearance of health, courtesy of several kilos of fruitcake that bulked up his skinny frame, and the contented, settled feeling that seeped up from his yellow soles. The feeling of well-being was compounded when he came home and found the crayons had soaked up the afternoon sun shining through the kitchen windows, and the room smelled of warm wax. Breathing it in made him feel warm and relaxed.

Cyrus didn't draw anything with the crayons. He just ran them over paper, filling up blank spaces, not creating as much as experiencing, falling back into the sensations of crayons between his fingers: the thick, slick feel of them, the way the wax flaked when he pressed too hard. It wasn't abstract. It wasn't anything. Just repetitive tactile stimulation. When he ran out of paper he drew over the sheets he did have, layers and layers of wax, until the crayons were stubs and the colors had blurred together and his hands were stained the same way as his soles.

The next day he bought more crayons. He thought, at first, of repeating that childhood limitation of color, of sticking to the yellows and blues and oranges and purples — the colors of sea stars and water and bruises — but in the end he got the lot, more for the bulk than anything else. It was a mistake. Melting the crayons produced a lot of wax, but the colors ran together, became unprepossessing, unsuitable for missing limbs. He dumped the first attempt and bought more crayons, went to a crafts store where they were sold separately instead of in packs. Cyrus bought entire bags of them, of yellow and blue and orange and purple crayons, and when he melted them, he made sure to do it in a separate pot for each color.

He melted the yellow first, spread greaseproof parchment paper over the dining table and upended the yellow wax pot. The wax was too hot to work with at first, but he spread it across the surface of the table so it cooled quicker. When it was cool enough to touch he separated it into equal pieces and shaped the pieces into petals. He threaded the petals one by one onto a length of flexible wire, and then wound that wire into great concentric circles of wax petals spiraling out, a deconstructed sunflower.

The orange crayons were melted and turned into a sea star. It was not whole. The sea star was wasting, disintegrating. The central body was there. It had retained a few arms. The rest of the arms were separate. Some of them were almost whole. Some of them were losing their shape, some of them had no shape at all. Cyrus remembered his mother making crème brûlée to impress special guests, proud of her facility with a blowtorch, and he found a small one in the baking aisle of a scullery shop, used it to sear the disintegrating arms into more interesting shapes, give them a slight liquid sheen from another melting. When the wax cooled a second time, he carved into the arms with a kitchen knife.

He was unsurprised to find that what he was carving, unconsciously at first, was apologies.

The blue crayons, melted, looked like deep ocean currents. Cyrus did less to them than to the others, rolling chunks of crayon into sea star arms and then rolling further, stretching them out as wasting disease stretched the arms of the sea stars. He twisted the end of each arm slightly, dug his thumbs into the twist until it made a little cup, and filled the crayon cups with sunflower seeds, pressed them into the warm, tacky crayon until they lined the cups and looked like toothy little mouths, ready and waiting to consume.

The purple crayons, the ones that when melted looked most like bruises, those he rolled and shaped and carved until they looked like a severed arm. It took a while to get the fingers right, before he stopped trying to recreate what he remembered from the letterbox and the fields and the fence and the porch and started using his own arm as a model. When he was done with the arm he didn't carve an apology into it. Instead, he studded the arm with sunflower seeds until he could hardly see the purple anymore.

He thought about leaving them on the kitchen table, to see if sunlight could made them shift and move and soften into different shapes, but Cyrus didn't want different shapes. He liked the shapes he had, and left them in the relative cool of the empty bathtub instead, so they could harden up, a rigor mortis of crayon, something he could enjoy a little longer.

When his colleagues noticed the smears of waxy color he'd missed on his skin, he smiled and told them it was art therapy. They were pleased for him, and he was pleased in turn that he had found a way to cope with the corpses in his garden, in his waters, the various dismemberments of his life. He'd known people who had succumbed to Grief, of course — everyone did — but he'd never been close to any of them and those he had known had always ended up, before the end, looking … unbalanced. As if the loss around them was causing them to lose themselves, and publicly.

He was grateful that wasn't happening to him.

"Honestly," said Jerry, "it reminds me of *Frankenstein.* You know, the bits where he's gathering dead people for parts. What happened to the pieces he didn't use, that's what I'd like to know."

"I don't think he dumped them in someone else's flower beds. The book would have said something about that, surely," said Cyrus.

"Yeah. Wasn't much on boundaries, that man."

"Perhaps he used them for other experiments. Couldn't have been easy, reanimating a whole person at once. Perhaps he practiced on the parts."

Cyrus wondered what Frankenstein would have thought of the living corpses of sea stars. Then he wondered what Mary Shelley would have thought of them. She had written *Frankenstein,* and part of the inspiration for it had been the experiments of Luigi Galvani, who had applied electricity to a dead frog in order to watch its back legs twitch. A grotesque experiment, but one that reminded him of sea stars, and the way their dismembered limbs continued to move after they had decayed enough to fall off their bodies. Those limbs had lives of their own, for a little while, as the bodies they had detached from withered and wasted. Likewise, the frog's legs exhibited twitches of life, muscles moving in dead flesh. No wonder such cause and effect had, in Shelley's book, been practiced on corpses. Cyrus would practice a great deal to be able to reanimate the dead, to create a better, stronger animation than the zombie half-life those limbs had now.

At least the dead arms left around his property weren't animated. Then he wondered if they could be.

He was glad when Jerry left.

Cyrus didn't sleep that night. He sat up in bed, propped against his headboard, with the bedside light on, holding one arm out in front of him. He flexed his fingers. He made a fist. Slowly, over and over again, watching the muscles move beneath the skin.

If I lost you, he thought, looking at his arm, *what would it take to bring you back to life again?* An electric current, to simulate the memory of life? Or a more lasting sort of transformation? *What would be enough?*

It was one thing to take terrible inspiration from the history of science, he thought, but surely *knowing* it was terrible was an indication that such inspiration came from curiosity, and not from Grief. Given recent events, lucidity was achievement enough, even without adding in the persistent pressure of the sea stars, the knowledge that if he couldn't help them then they'd quietly disintegrate beneath the surface of the waters, until there was nothing recognizable left of them. Those beautiful, brilliant sea stars. What incalculable loss it would be.

Surely, if he were in the shallows of Grief and heading for the drop off, he would look at his arm and see one of theirs. It would be a question of association: the dismemberment in the sunflower fields, the dismemberment of the sea stars. It was reasonable to conflate them, to expect the human limbs to twitch and crawl after their severing, in the same way the sea star arms did — or if not to expect, then to imagine. The images were too similar, and underlining that similarity was the expression of regret. His, for the sea stars, and the regret of the person who took those arms, who decorated them with apologies and left them for Cyrus to find.

Lately, what he most seemed to regret was that the arms left on the borders of his home were taken away again. It had almost become routine … the discovery, the call to the police, the arrival and examination and removal. The way that people looked at him sideways, the surveillance vehicles parked across the street. Not that they ever picked anything up, and Cyrus had vetoed motion-activated floodlights on his property. It was pointed out to him this indicated a lack of desire stop whatever butchery had him at its center, but the thought of that artificial sunlight was unpleasant. He didn't want replacements for sunshine, or for sea stars. He wanted them the way they were, whole and in their proper place.

He didn't know when he began to consider his home the proper place for dismemberment, but night after night of sitting up in bed and calculating the movement of his own arms had convinced him that he was edging closer to a rather more vivid experience of it. His body smelled of wax enough already.

If I suspect that I am falling into Grief, he thought, *is that rationality, or is it just fear?*

If it was the former, that could only be a contraindication, surely. He felt rational. His work wasn't suffering, if a continual failure to remedy the wasting disease constituted "not suffering." His colleagues felt sorry for him, but the suspicion was gone, and Cyrus was pretty sure they'd say he was sane. The fact that they believed he was in therapy, and that he was rational enough to ask for help with what could only be a traumatic experience was a point in his favor. His relationship with his family was good. He had friends. Jerry was a regular visitor. That the therapy was self-administered shouldn't count against him. It seemed to be working. Intrusive thoughts about the loss of his own arm were only that: intrusive, and intruders could be kept out.

Or, if not kept out, welcomed in on very specific terms.

Crayons had worked well enough, the wax sculptures allowing him to face up to the similarities between vocation and victimhood.

Someone was leaving him arms, and his work was about the loss of them. Wax explained nothing, but did allow him to accept the link. Perhaps a different mimicry would do more.

3: *Love*

Cyrus found himself researching prosthetic arms.

"I'd ask, but I don't think I want to know," said Jerry. "This is just wallowing, this is."

"I'm not wallowing. It's only ... I don't know who these people are. All I know about them is their parts, and a person's more than parts. Look, I'm under no illusions here. The people who lost these arms are probably dead. I know I haven't been sympathetic to the idea of a serial killer, but the only way I can think to explain this is that someone's taken them and killed them and cut them up, and the arms end up here. And by the time they end up here, there's nothing can be done for them. The police are doing their best but the owners of those arms are dead, and if they're not the arms can't be reattached now, can they?" They'd been separated too long, kept in fields of flowers instead of an ice box, the decomposition process gone on too long. "But I can't help but think there might be people out there without an arm who need one."

Cyrus tapped at his phone and brought up a fundraiser for a little girl who had been born without an arm.

Jerry took the phone, scrolled down, and sighed heavily. "I guess I can spare a few dollars. Is that what you're doing? Donating?"

"It seems like a way to make something positive out of this," Cyrus admitted.

It was the truth, if not all of it. Support of charities, reaching out to help others, that was normal. Respectable. No one suffering from Grief would do that. He didn't need to research the different types of prosthetic arms to be charitable, though. Yet charity, Cyrus admitted, was also an excuse.

Did Marjorie have excuses of her own? he wondered. *Did she have ways to make herself look normal, until she couldn't anymore? When the Grief first came for her, did she know she had it? Did she try to bargain with it, keep her sanity for as long as she could?*

"Getting any further with the sea stars?" Jerry asked. "Because, you know, there's opportunity here. What with the aquarium and all. If I were you I'd hold a fundraiser."

"For the kid or the sea stars?"

"For both."

"Isn't that a bit tacky?" Cyrus asked. "Morbid, even, considering I'm the one who'd end up running it?"

"Guy who owns the dumping ground for severed arms gives arms back," said Jerry. "Helping hands. Makes a great headline. Yeah, it's morbid, but morbid might work for you here."

"That child's parents won't want her associated with true crime and zombies."

"That child's parents are holding bake sales so their kid can have a shot at a normal life. They might be more open than you think. And by open, I mean desperate."

"No one's going to agree to this," said Cyrus.

Everyone agreed to it. As an event, it came together a lot quicker than he expected. And Jerry was right, morbidity sold. Elizabeth, the child without an arm, came dressed as zombie. "She *loves* zombies," said her mother. "Creepy things. I don't know where she gets it from." Together, they watched Elizabeth lurk and lurch around the aquarium tanks, groaning "*Braiiins*" at all the guests, though she took special delight in groaning at the people who, like herself, had come in zombie costume. There were lots of them. Some were even dressed as zombie sea stars, with little arms half-attached with nylon and dragging behind, as if in the process of disintegrating.

"This is the most tasteless thing I've ever seen in my life," said Jerry. "Good job. Tasteless pays."

Did it ever.

"Something to tell your accountant friends," Cyrus replied.

"You'd think so, wouldn't you," said Jerry, and in his voice there was a bitter, wistful undertone Cyrus would remember later and wonder at.

Both Cyrus and Elizabeth's dad gave a talk; the first about wasting disease, the second about disability. Elizabeth was supposed to say a few words as well, but enamored as she was of the zombie costume, even the most persuasive journalist couldn't get anything out of her but "*Braiiins.*" Still, as a group they were sympathetic, and the event raised enough for a new arm for Elizabeth and a new tank to help support the sea stars.

It was gratifying to be able to help, but facilitating prosthetic arms for others wasn't enough. Cyrus wanted his own. Something more realistic, and less malleable, than crayon. Second-hand shops were initially helpful. There he found old dress dummies, the models that stood in department store windows, their plastic arms detachable. They were also jointed, some of them, and if the joints weren't always working then Cyrus could oil them, fix them up, although the results were limited. Taken off at the shoulder, they would, at most, be hinged at the elbow. The fingers were a mold of undifferentiated plastic, shaped to give the impression of hands but nothing close to reality. Still, they were good enough.

He took one of the arms, and painted it carefully with nail polish. It was the same bright yellow he'd used on his toenails. He layered coat after coat with the same small brush and hung the arm from the porch to dry. Not ten minutes later there was a knock at his door. The police from the surveillance van across the street come to investigate. When Cyrus showed them it was a plastic replica from a department store model, they'd looked at him with utter bemusement. "Are you trying to make yourself look like a suspect?" one of them asked him.

"Are you trying to make yourself look like a lunatic?" Jerry said. "Is this trauma-induced insanity or something like that?"

"It's art therapy," said Cyrus. "It's abstract."

"It's a load of bullshit is what it is," said Jerry. "I'm afraid one day I'll turn up here and you'll have cut your own arm off."

"Sorry," said Cyrus.

He never meant for people to worry. He was just trying to get by. It wasn't easy, devoting himself to a species on the brink, one that was dying, horrifically, before his eyes. The starvation, the withering. The way their arms twisted before they fell off, the way they writhed once the dismemberment was done. And then the final disintegration, into shapeless flesh, without even the dignity of an unmutilated death. He tried not to wonder if it hurt them, the sea stars, to die that way.

He couldn't believe it was painless.

Dissolving couldn't be painless either. The injection of vinegar, an acid wash from the inside out. It must have felt like burning alive. If someone injected him with acid, he'd die screaming. And it was an extraordinary thing, the Great Barrier Reef, an ecology built of marvel as well as coral, but was it worth saving if the price was such uninhibited sadism? He pictured his sea stars there, the bright, enormous sunflowers of them spread over the coral. He pictured them falling apart, and screaming. He pictured the crown-of-thorns in the colder waters of the north Pacific, and himself hovering over them underwater, syringes in his hands.

He wrote a postcard to Marjorie. *You deserve what happened to you. I hope Grief hurts.* Then he stuck the postcard on his fridge with the picture side out, a generic beach scene, because he didn't know where to send it now that she'd left the university. It probably wasn't a good idea to have it traced back to him anyway. Yet seeing it on the fridge day after day, knowing the words behind the picture and not being able to express them, ate away at him. He bought plain envelopes, professional envelopes, and sealed the postcard into one of them, then drove two hours to a neighboring city and posted it there, with no return address. On the front of the envelope he wrote Marjorie's name, and the department at her university. They might be able to forward her mail. Their problem if they couldn't. It was enough for him to send it. But having sent one, he couldn't stop the rest.

It's a monstrous thing you did. As good as murder.

Perhaps Grief only affects the really guilty. Have you thought of that?

Do you think they screamed when they died? Do you think you will?

I'm glad you're going to die.

Why don't you just kill yourself?

The anonymity was soothing. He'd never have been able to say any of that to her face. To anyone's face. That wasn't Grief; that was self-preservation. Anyone who'd spent any time online knew people could be vicious when they had a screen to hide behind. He used pen and paper — so what?

Marjorie probably wouldn't get the cards anyway. If she did, she'd have tipped so far over into insanity that it wouldn't have mattered. And if that was guilt, the thought of kicking a sick woman when she was down, well. Perhaps he wouldn't have his own sanity to hide behind much longer.

A thin film of vinegar, spread over his arm, tingled a little. Mostly it just covered the smell of crayon. A shallow cut made with the same knife he used to carve *I'm sorry* into wax. The vinegar stung when applied to that — a thin, high-pitched pain that would burst a millionfold into veins, searing them, collapsing them. Dissolving them from the inside out.

Those poor starfish, he thought. *Even if they were monsters, they didn't deserve that.*

One day one of the postcards came back. It was in a plain envelope, similar to the ones he had posted himself, with his own name on it. It was the postcard which read *Why don't you just kill yourself?*

Beneath it, Marjorie had scrawled just one word.

Yes.

He rang her old university, and spoke to one of her colleagues. The woman was a friend of Marjorie's, and she had been crying.

"Yes," she said.

He didn't ask how she'd done it. It didn't matter, and Cyrus could picture any number of ways. The nightmares continued, him in a wetsuit, hands full of needles, the meaty sensation of stabbing something that both was and wasn't starfish. Him in fields of sunflowers, watering the ground with vinegar, watching the flowers wither around him. He sent another postcard, knowing it would never be read.

I don't forgive you.

It was, perhaps, the kindest letter he'd ever sent to her. After all, if he knew anything, he knew in the marrow of his unvinegared bones that Marjorie didn't forgive herself either. Even postmortem, she'd probably have enjoyed his agreement.

If someone had rubbed her face in the loss of the Reef by leaving dead chunks of coral in her garden? Cyrus bet, on some level, she would have enjoyed that too.

Part of him was glad she was dead. It might have been his fault, at least a little — though what was fault in the face of Grief? His callousness had contributed. In being so callous, he had been — and it was an almost-pleasure to admit it — *effective.*

He had yearned so long for effectiveness.

2: Creativity, again

The painted model arm from the department store wasn't enough. It was too yellow, too flat. Too lacking in texture. It seemed less like an arm than a vehicle for nail polish. While the polish was lovely, and reminded him of sunflowers, it looked better on living things — or at least those things that had more of a resemblance to the living, either in appearance or in texture.

Cyrus began to re-create. Mimicry was resemblance, he thought, but it could also be camouflage. It could also be understanding.

He had to buy a new letterbox. In deference to his friend, he kept his post office box as well, because the letterbox was never going to be used for mail, and he suspected Jerry would never use it anyway. The new letterbox was identical to the old one. Cyrus took one of his spare model arms and painted it yellow, like he did the first one, but this time he dipped the shoulder end, where the joint would have been, in melted crayon. The blues and purples reminded him of ocean currents and decomposition and bruising. He made a tag from cardboard and old string and tied it around the wrist, but this time the tag didn't say *I'm sorry*. This time, the tag said *Pycnopodia helianthoides*, the scientific name of the sunflower sea star. Useful information, and far less intrusive, lacking as it did even the smallest plea for forgiveness.

When he stuffed the arm into the letterbox, the tag facing outward, he knew that whenever he opened the letterbox he would see sunflowers.

The second arm was smaller, more delicate, and Cyrus was intending to paint it yellow as well, but when he thought about what he wanted to do to the nails he changed his mind. He painted it a dark blue, with a nail polish flecked with gold sparkles. Then, carefully, he painted bright yellow sea stars on each nail. He had to practice beforehand, with a smaller brush than that which came with the nail polish, but the sea stars, when they were done, were at least recognizable. He left it on the porch, in front of the door; he had to step over it whenever he left the house for work, and when he came home. It was a constant reminder to look where he was going, and at what he was doing.

The third he painted the same dark blue, but instead of the apology tattoo he etched a sea star into the surface of the arm with a knife, the long triangular arms separate from the central body, a stylized deconstruction. He cut deep into the plastic and the knife broke through the surface of the arm. He filled the hollow with earth and sunflower seeds and left the arm in the fields to sprout.

He painted a sea star on the palm of the fourth arm. The fifth he smashed to bits. The plastic pieces were painted yellow and rolled in salt while they were still wet, and Cyrus hung them from the sunflowers with strings, so that whenever he walked through the fields he could smell the faint scent of ocean. The sixth was a collection of arms, bolted together where the shoulders would have been, and the hands splayed outwards like the spokes of a wheel. He nailed the whole contraption to the top of the fence, and left seeds in all of the palms. He would have liked to find a way for the arms to fall off the bolts, one by one, scattering seeds as they fell, but the mechanism was too much for him and instead he set it on top of the fence post, where it could spin in the wind.

The rest he stippled, as if they were sea stars, trying to make them as life-like as he could, and planting them in the fields, red and orange and yellow, all the arms separate from each other.

"Art therapy," he said to Jerry, when he confronted Cyrus about his garden decorations. "Art therapy," he said to Melissa, when Jerry took photos on his phone and sent them to his mother, along with a request for her fruitcake recipe. "Art therapy," he said to his colleagues at the aquarium. "I'm trying to cope with what happened."

Mostly, he was trying to cope with the fact that the severed arms seemed to have stopped appearing. He'd go for days, for weeks, without finding more of them. The police had packed up their surveillance.

With little activity left to monitor their focus had shifted to more immediate carnage: the people setting themselves alight for protest, the continuation of old refusals under new Grief. The arms' absence should have made him feel relieved. Instead, Cyrus felt abandoned, as if he'd been amputated from the common body.

"Why are you doing this to me?" he said, on the porch at night. "What have I ever done to you, but try to help?" There was no one listening. He didn't know who he was talking to. He thought it might have been the sea stars, but there were less and less of them, and they never understood him anyway.

"What do you *want*?" he said. "I'd help you if I could."

But every day he was alone, more helplessly adrift in a sea of sacrifice and shifting sanity. Immolation was only the latest symptom of the latest hopelessness. Cyrus didn't like to think about those poor, charred histories, and it was easier to look away. He wasn't the only one to do so. Media coverage was limited.

Grief was contagious enough without attention lighting yet another match.

The wasting disease had spread to the aquarium. Cyrus didn't know how; nobody knew how. The sea stars should have been safe there, away from the waters of their home. Wasting disease had ravaged stocks held in institutions before — captive populations held in zoos and other aquaria were not exempt. Antibiotics were supposed to help, and had in the past, but when Cyrus got into the tanks himself, dived to the bottom and hovered above the sea stars, he could barely administer the drug without shaking. Looking at the needle, his only thought was *Please don't let this be vinegar*. It made no sense. He'd checked the syringe contents a dozen times over. He *knew* they contained antibiotics, but the fear remained.

The sea stars stopped eating, no matter what he tried to tempt them with. They shriveled in on themselves. Their limbs twisted and elongated, began to rot on their bodies and detach in the tanks. Cyrus dived for the pieces, cupped the wobbling, arm-shaped jelly in his palms and kicked for the surface, for sterilization and microscopes and tissue samples that told him nothing he didn't already know.

He knew he shouldn't have done it — that it wouldn't make a difference, wouldn't be a comfort, and might actually be a contagion — but he couldn't help it. Each time he dived for pieces of sea star, for administration of antibiotic, with small meaty treats they refused to eat, he found himself stroking the sickly, shivering bodies of the sea stars, trying to instill in them his own strength, the depth of the love he had for them, and how they weren't alone in their suffering. He watched their deaths, dragged out over days, over weeks, and wondered if, in the end, the vinegar might have been kinder.

He wrote another postcard to a dead woman, and sent it.

Is this what desperation feels like?

And another. And another.

I'm sorry. I'm sorry.

So sorry.

As if the apologies would do any good. Offering them didn't make him feel better, which was what apologies were most often supposed to do: placate the guilt of the apologist. He kept making them anyway. Partly out of habit, partly because he meant them, but mostly because he *wanted* to mean them more than he did, and wanted them to be made meaningful even if they weren't.

Marjorie had apologized to him once. He wished she hadn't bothered; it was resentment on his part, resentment coloring the past, but at times he felt as if that apology had been bait. Drawing him back into their conversation, making him complicit in a death that hadn't come yet.

At home, the sunflowers withered in the fields. The stems buckled, the petals shrank to ragged, dirty fragments, their color spoiled.

"Everything's dying," he said.

"You're working too much. You've forgotten to water them, that's all" said Jerry. He'd come over with takeaways, in a transparent excuse to get Cyrus to eat something, and he rummaged in the kitchen cupboards for clean plates. "When was the last time you did the washing up?"

"Why do you even care?"

"I'm worried about you," said Jerry. "And I'm worried about me too. I was unhappy in my old life so I changed it. Changed everything. Didn't plan to. Thought I'd keep my mates. But it turned out they weren't my friends; they were just people I worked with. And when I wasn't around to go to lunch, or drinks after work, well. I'm lonely. Then you and your bloody letterbox ... it was something that happened to the both of us that no one else understood. It felt like having a friend again. Which is great, but you've got no sense of self-preservation. So, you know. I hang around because I like you. I bring you dinner because I like you. I don't have that many mates left I can afford to see one starve."

Cyrus stared at him. "That's the worst guilt trip I've ever heard."

Jerry shrugged. "Your mother suggested it. We've been corresponding. She likes my granny's scone recipe. She's trying to teach me about pastry."

"Don't make her plum pie," said Cyrus, automatically.

"I did. It's dreadful."

"Fucking awful. Worse than fruitcake."

"I like that fruitcake," said Jerry. "Eat your dinner."

Cyrus ate. Then he did the washing up while Jerry went out and uncoiled the hose amidst the sunflowers. Cyrus came home, more and more, to find his old postman in his sunflower fields, watering. Jerry said he saw a difference, but Cyrus wasn't convinced. The sunflowers blurred together, blurred into sea stars, and sometimes he dreamed in the night that his own arms were sunflower stems, that his reaching hands were sunflowers themselves, or that his fingers were formed from sea stars, and dropping off one by one in his bed. He woke scrambling for the lights, ripping the covers off the bed, searching for his own dead fingers scattered over sheets until his heartbeat calmed and he could see his hands, still whole, still attached.

"You need a holiday," said his mother. "Your friend's right. You're working too hard."

"There's too much to do," said Cyrus, thinking of how many sea stars would die if he wasn't at the aquarium. He ignored the knowledge that the number would be the same either way. When his boss made it clear a day off was required, in his case, he went along because it was better than arguing. Arguing might earn him a lengthier absence. Instead, he drove two hours to the city where he'd sent his anonymous postcards. This time, he didn't have any postcards. He didn't know what there was left to say. He sat alone in a cafe, trying not to cry, before he was convinced that the effort was a waste, and got his coffee to go. He drank it in a park, sitting on a bench hidden half behind hedges, where no one could see him and he wouldn't be a bother and it didn't matter to anyone if he were sobbing into a paper cup full of an indifferent blend that he didn't want anyway.

When someone sat suddenly beside him, Cyrus tried to pull himself together. The last thing he needed was solicitous inquiry, the kind questioning that might lead to a diagnosis he could not accept and had worked hard to prevent. He scrubbed his hands over his face and stared at his lap, trying to regulate his breathing. He didn't see the handkerchief until it was offered to him.

"Thanks," he said. "Sorry about this." It was automatic, that apology. He didn't actually mean it, or at least he thought he didn't. Most of the time, he couldn't tell. Apologies had become shorthand for actions he was unwilling to commit to.

Looking up, not because he wanted to but because eye contact was polite, he saw that the young woman who had given him her handkerchief had only one arm. He couldn't help it; his eyes dropped to her nails, remembering the careful manicure, the perfectly centered letters of *SORRY*.

Her nails were clean and unpainted. Even so, she looked familiar to him, somehow familiar, but it wasn't until she spoke that he was able to place her: the woman he'd met the first time he'd bought nail polish. The woman with a friend who'd lost her arm, and who had now lost her own in turn.

"Is this what you're looking for?" she said, and held her hand out, as if to offer a handshake, before rotating her wrist so that her hand was palm up. On that palm, spreading petals along the underside of her fingers, was a sunflower.

"It's only paint," she said. "A friend did it for me. I've been thinking about getting it tattooed there. It's more permanent. I'm afraid of the pain, though."

"I had the bottom of my feet done," said Cyrus. "It hurt like a bitch. At the time I thought it was a stabilizing pain. It doesn't seem that way now."

"Maybe you didn't go far enough," said the woman. Her name, she told him, was Elizabeth. "Or it might as well be." The same name as the little girl who'd only ever had one arm, who Cyrus had helped to raise money for.

"I don't get to know your real name?"

"Do you want to?"

Cyrus considered. "I don't know," he said. "If I knew your real name, I'd have to do something about it, wouldn't I?" Then again, she was a fellow human being. Perhaps he was obligated, even if she wanted to be anonymous. "Are you alright? Do you need help?"

Elizabeth looked at him and laughed. "Why would I need help?" she said. "I'm not the one crying in a park. If you don't mind my saying so, you look worse than I do." It was the absolute truth. Aside from the absence of arm, she looked rested and glossy. Shining eyes, shining hair. No lines on her face, no indication of trauma, and she was so much lighter than the unhappy woman he'd met in the store. So much happier.

"Someone left an arm in my sunflower fields," said Cyrus. "Rather a lot of arms, actually. I'm pretty sure one of them is yours."

"It is," said Elizabeth.

"I thought you were probably dead. The rest of you, anyway. I thought it was a serial killer. That sounds dramatic, I know. But there was a severed arm stuffed into my letterbox. I think I'm forgiven a little drama."

"Drama, yes. But don't you think you've been a little obtuse? Serial killers, really. Did it truly never cross your mind that it might have been voluntary?"

Voluntary.

"I used to be a diver," she said. "I loved it. The coolness of the water, the way it slipped around me. The world that lived beneath the surface. When I started diving it was abundant, and then it wasn't. The worst of it was the sea stars. I stopped diving so I wouldn't have to see them fall apart, but then they started washing up on beaches, pieces of them, and I couldn't even have that anymore. Couldn't walk along the beach, couldn't even get my feet wet. And I'm not a scientist. I failed my science classes at school. I work in a bakery. There was nothing I could do."

The sun was behind her, a halo shining through her hair, and it was so bright Cyrus couldn't look at her directly. If he squinted, the absence of her left arm wasn't total after all. If he squinted, he could almost see it had been replaced with sea star. That she'd made them part of her, like they were part of him, but different. Then a cloud passed over the sun, a temporary shadow, and the illusion receded. It was just absence. Just a human absence.

"I wanted to be able to do something," said Elizabeth. "I wasn't the only one." She reached out her one hand and clasped both of his own, the sunflower of her palm pressed against his flesh. "Sometimes the only thing you can do, against the horror of the world, is sacrifice," she said. "Did you think you were the only one who loved them?"

Cyrus had never thought that. Secretly, though, he'd thought he was the only one who loved them enough. He'd never considered that other people might love them more. Even if that more was ... twisted, somehow, into a calculus of Grief, that said *I will give of myself to save you*. Even if the saving was hopeless, because science didn't work like that. It didn't run on atonement. It didn't take love into account, or sacrifice.

"It's not enough," he said. "The wasting sickness ... it's in the aquarium now. You know I work in an aquarium?"

"I know. All of us know."

All those arms, offering up. All those alms, atoning.

"The antibiotics aren't working. Whatever it is has mutated. I've ordered a different type but they're dying, and there's nothing I can do. I've tried everything I know, I've held them in my hands and they fall apart. They're still moving and they don't know they're dead. They're disintegrating in their tanks. They're wasting. They're starving."

"You can help them."

"I don't know how," said Cyrus.

"Yes, you do."

And he did. It was alchemy, not science, that made him think of solutions: the strange and pitiful alchemy of Grief.

"Sometimes I wonder," said Elizabeth, staring at the single palm she had left, the one painted over with sunflower. "If it's really a sunflower I should have here. Sometimes I think it should be a flame."

Immolation in the face of systemic injustice, the burnings that hardly anyone mentioned. When Cyrus saw the brief references to them on the news, he changed the channel.

"No one pays attention to flames anymore," he said. They were too common, and too useless.

Barely worth the apology.

⁂

He had a key to the aquarium and let himself in after hours. He had sunflowers and vinegar. He had yellow ribbons for a tourniquet, and nail polish, and knives. He had the crayon arm he'd created, hardened from hours spent in the bathtub and then the fridge and studded with sunflower seeds. He'd filled himself with fruitcake, for love and for strength.

He couldn't make the cuts himself. None of them could. None of them had. Elizabeth had given him a number, and Cyrus had called it, and the person who came to him was veiled. Cyrus was glad for that. He wanted perfect anonymity. He wanted to look at people on the street, afterwards, and imagine they had been the ones to help him. His arm was injected with anesthetic, and Cyrus lay back on sunflowers in front of the tanks and gripped the shapeless crayon hand with the fingers he was keeping. He pressed his forehead against the glass. The sea stars were on the other side, failing. Fading and sick, pieces of them falling off, unwilling to feed. He'd injected them with the new antibiotic, but he no longer believed it would be enough. The warming waters, the patterns of behavior society had refused to change so creatures like the sea stars could survive ... nothing as bloodless as antibiotic could make up for that.

He'd bathed his arm in vinegar. He'd written the apology, barely worth it, on the inside of his wrist. He'd painted the sunflower on his palm. Behind the glass, another arm fell off. A sunflower arm, twitching.

They lost their arms together. His sacrifice a reflection in the glass, twitching. He wasn't Frankenstein, using electricity to resurrect the dead. He'd chosen sympathy instead.

The person who had removed his arm left, still veiled, and Cyrus' arm was on the floor beside him. It lay on sunflowers, their petals sticky and red. Cyrus had thought he might feel fuzzy afterwards, the shock seeded through him like sunflower heads, but it had been a mistake, all along, to think that Grief was a vehicle for sorrow. The only thing it brought, the only thing it ever brought, was clarity.

He dropped his severed arm into the tank and leaned against the glass, waiting for them to feed. Waiting for the sea stars to drag the ruin of their mutilated bodies across sand and onto flesh. Waited for them to know that they were loved, and they no longer needed to waste, because there were those who would give of themselves so the sea stars could survive.

Cyrus was certain they would.

With his one hand, he took out his cell phone and dialed, his fingers shaking. "Jerry?" he said, when his friend picked up. "Are you there?"

Our Flesh was Bred for This

Death is different for island folk.

It's an old saying, if not a truthful one. There are islands enough for carnivores. On Kodiak they stake you out for bears, on Komodo you're left for dragons. Not everywhere is barren of hunting teeth. In most places they've come back, feed them up so carefully as we do.

But there are some islands where they never were. Islands of birds and bats, and the only big carnivores are marine, their fish-bellies white around the coast, their easy length swum up along estuaries and into rivers. The great hinged jaw of leopard seals, the smooth sleek lines of blackfish.

Apex predators, all of them.

That our bodies float face down until sheared apart instead of lying with our faces to the sun, our bellies split open, well. Death is different for island folk, and people who spend their lives in scent and sight of sea make their plans accordingly.

It's such a careful, chancy thing. Such a wistful thing, the thought of afterlife and salt, for the sea can't take us all, and we have to fight for place.

There's people don't desire it. Who think themselves more than meat and want a cemetery death, the way old generations went out, using up land cleared of trees and filling the soil with formaldehyde, the remnant chemicals of embalming, as if what we did with pesticides and microplastics wasn't enough. We kept killing even after we died, our bodies a reminder of the apocalypse we'd brought.

There's no waste like that now, not even for all the dead who want to go back.

Apex predators die the same as other beasts. They can feed the same as others, too.

A chancy thing, a careful thing. We want to see them back, those populations we broke down. Death and climate, death and habitat loss, death and poison all around, and by the end the only species relied upon to swarm was us. Well, there were insects. Bacteria, too, all the small creatures. The herbivores hung on the longest, but when we think of challenge, of the ones that stalk through imagination and make mirrors of our acts it's the carnivores we think of, the fearful symmetry of our other selves.

They were so very hard to feed.

But there were so many of us, and so few of them. A simple equation, an obvious solution. Something had to be done with us. And cemeteries were wasted land that was better off reclaimed, crematoria were air pollution and wasted fuel.

People donate their bodies all the time, or used to. Those bodies went to science once, spread out and skinned by medical students, left fallow in a field for monitored decomposition. It was being eaten by worms then, by blowflies and all the other insects and for cause.

Better the body goes to feeding something with a bit more brilliance to it, a bit more beauty.

But it takes so much care. As much meat as we are, as much mechanism of flesh, there's so many of us. It's one thing to support the food web, another to unbalance it entirely. No one wants to feed themselves to rats, to encourage a population explosion as destructive as our own. We've only begun to clear the land of what we brought.

But death is different for island folk, and when we let the dead slide into waters off Stewart Island, naked and empty of poison, fed to fish the size of funeral boats, we give them time to recover. Not just the fish, the but seals they would have eaten if our flesh wasn't offered up as ransom.

The seal colonies are recovering now as well. For a little while at least their predators have easier food, if not so fat. In other places there are antelopes again, herds of them building up because our pride has given way to another, because our bodies atone in death for what our brains have done. The vultures, the eagles, all the loveliness we pushed to extinction now bury their beaks in our entrails and it is good.

We weaned ourselves from ecosystem once, or said we did. But death is different for island folk, and we do not go into it entire, or alone.

Tidemarks

I never expected to see them.

The arrogance of it, the pride — as if seeing or not seeing made any sort of difference. But I had a reason, so I thought, and that made me better than the people who came through here with lamplights and laughter, expecting the echoes of creatures long gone, mistaking phosphorescence for phantoms. Not that there was much of that, even, but in the middle of the night, with atmosphere and poor light ... people see what they want to. And I wanted to see the dead so badly.

I could see them so easily in daylight. They're all there, on the upper floors of the Otago museum, dead birds behind glass with hard little eyes, figures fluffed out with stuffing and the feathers smoothed down so that the colors blended into one another, and softly. Artifacts of extinction.

"You know you can see them for real," Lucy says. "Out at the old marine lab in Portobello, where the aquarium used to be." It's a story I've heard as well — one of those things that gets passed down and down through the marine science department, a faculty folk tale. That late at night, when the ocean's very still and the tide is at its highest point, the penguins come back.

They've been gone for decades. When fish stocks collapsed the sea birds went with them. The penguins, the albatross at Taiaroa ... some of the gulls managed to hang on, but then they've always been scavengers.

Lucy's determined that the stories are true. I don't believe it. Wishful thinking, and why would penguins come to an aquarium they never lived at? I've been to that lab, abandoned as it is and no longer fit for purpose. I've walked through its ruins — the aquarium, too. The tanks are empty, the glass broken. Stones in the tanks to account for the shattering. I can't say that I threw any myself — there wasn't exactly a lot of glass left to shatter, less lingering respect than lack of opportunity — but I felt the temptation. The place was such a wreck. Just an echoing emptiness, and the outside tanks, more like swimming pools, had standing puddles in the bottom, scummed over and full of sandflies. The whole place in shades of grey and rose, the tidemarks pink and rising.

"Come on," Lucy says. "Call yourself a scientist. Think of it as an experiment."

"In gullibility?" I ask her, and it's a flippant response. Lucy considers it anyway.

"In hope, perhaps," she says. "I hear it comes with feathers."

Better feathers than red tides, I suppose.

✹

Truth was I'd heard the legend before I even got to the university. Knew it to be true, as well. I'd seen them when I was a kid: those ghostly shapes, come out of water and waddling. Not what you'd expect of ghosts, nothing elegant about them. No trailing mists, no delicate movement. Just bodies ill-shaped for land, awkward in their stride but limned, just a little, in light that didn't come from stars, and didn't come from plankton, either. I'd say that's when I knew that I'd end up in conservation, but that would be a lie. I didn't know until I joined the marine science department and heard the stories about the ghosts, and who could see them.

"No one but scientists," says Lucy. "No one but biologists. That's us." But biology wasn't enough — it was love that brought sight with it. The determination to love something that was gone, to look at lack and choose to love it anyway. You don't have to be a scientist for that. But when love seeps through into *devotion*, when it becomes such a focus for life that the wish to preserve comes above everything else ...

It's obsession that leads to ghosts. Obsession and nothing else.

Lucy's halfway there already. No one wants to spend time at the old aquarium. Not even kids, who were probably the ones who broke those empty tanks in the first place. The whole building's just high up enough on the peninsula that the rising tides haven't swallowed it up, but the algal blooms that come with warming waters slop up against those outside pools, paint them red with toxicity and deoxygenated waters. Under moonlight the red tides are black, but under all light they are sticky and soft and carry the scent of rot. It seems almost cruel to watch for ghosts when they have to surface into that, into what climate and run-off have made of the waters that were once their home.

Whatever wonder there is in watching the dead rise out of the sea at the foundations of aquarium, there is little wonder in seeing them suffocate there, as if reborn into oil slicks. Albatross, falling with those wide, white wings into an ocean the color of blood and never rising again, penguins searching along shorelines for fish until their little starved bodies wash up, stained with red and dissolving in sand, as if they were never there at all.

"There's nothing there to see." That's what I tell Lucy. She doesn't believe me. The ghosts are calling her, she says, but an invitation is something which can be refused.

She wants to see absence for herself. I can't say that I let her, because it's not my place to grant permission, she's a grown woman, and she can make her own decision. Mine is that I don't have to go with her.

(Lucy goes, and she doesn't come back. She cut her throat on a shattered piece of aquarium glass, and this is added to the folk tale, between lectures and around water coolers: that the ghosts came for her, and now she haunts there too.)

(Lucy goes and comes back. There's a new streak of grey in her hair and she dyes it red, bright red, and then one day she can't stand looking at herself in the mirror and shaves it all off. "There was nothing there worth seeing," she says.)

(Lucy goes and comes back and everything is fine. "I guess it's just a silly story," she says, and there's disappointment in her face and I don't tell her that this is the best that can be hoped for, that she got off lucky, and that there are still the museum birds, behind unbroken glass and perfect.)

That is what ghosts do. They open up possibilities, they bring you face to face with things you don't *want* to face, and there's no guarantee of how you'll react when you see them.

"What would you do if you saw a ghost?" Lucy asks me, before she went out to try and find ghosts of her own. As if there were so many possibilities open for me, as if I hadn't narrowed them down and down until there was only one left.

Turn away. That's what I did. "It's just a silly story," I said. "Nothing there worth seeing." I went out to see ghosts and I didn't come back. There could have been grey, but I've always dyed my hair so who could tell, really.

What *would* I do if I saw a ghost?

It's a question that's been answered already. I lied about it. That seemed like the best thing to do. I know people say that children are truthful in some fundamental way, more so than adults, but that too is a lie. Children are good at imagination, and at invention, and they recreate the world around them to make it understandable. To make it palatable, I think. That's what I did, anyway. I sneaked out to the aquarium in the middle of the night, because I'd heard that it was haunted and I wanted to see ghosts.

More accurately, I wanted to see birds. If the penguins had been alive I'd have gone during the day, because the shops would have been open then and I could have bought some ice cream and eaten it all up while I was waiting for them to come out of surf and up onto sand. Not a romantic reason, perhaps, but I was not a romantic child. It didn't matter that they were ghosts. It mattered that they were penguins, and if the only way I could see penguins was behind glass in a museum or behind death on the coast, well ... it was easier to pretend the latter was living than the former.

The aquarium had been a broken, empty place. If I'd been interested in ghosts for the sake of ghosts it would have seemed a fine place for them. Atmospheric. There was broken glass, of course, pieces of detritus scattered round. The place had looked like a dump, but beneath the emptiness and the absence I could still see the clean lines where the tanks had been, the displays on the walls that had said which tank contained sea urchins and which contained starfish, which held crabs and black coral and cod.

One of the tanks was still intact. There was nothing in it, of course — all the inhabitants taken out, all the water drained away. The only thing left was dust. I'd drawn a happy face in it, and the awkward shape of a penguin which only illustrated why science, and not art, had been even then my preferred choice of career. If it had been a different world, with different waters, there might have been a phosphorescent glow to follow the trace of fingers ... plankton and bright colors and presence, but those things don't belong in empty buildings and empty tanks, so I'd dismissed the brief small spark as a trick of the light, a reflection from the torch I'd brought with me, and not a ghost at all.

I'd decided all the ghosts were outside, you see. That was how the story went. Penguins and albatross and the red surface of water, algal blooms and old blood. I left the tanks behind and went outside, with the aquarium at my back, and looked to the waters and expected the ghosts to come.

And they did.

It was awful. Unbearable. And more than anything, hopeless.

That's the thing about ghost stories. There's supposed to be a *reason* that the ghost is doing what it's doing. Even a kid like me, who'd never read a whole lot of ghost stories, knew there was supposed to be a reason. Ghosts came so that people could find their bodies. They came to pass on a message. They came to get vengeance on those who had killed them. And once you figured out what they wanted, you could make them go away, and it would be a good thing, helping them pass on.

There was no good thing about the aquarium's dead. They washed up in waves, they came to settle on water and sank there. They thrashed and suffered and died like they'd died the first time, and those of them that made it out of the ocean and onto the dark little sliver of beach, well. They stumbled in the memory and presence of algae, they smothered in tides. And there was no reason for it, because there were too many bodies to find and there was nothing that they could tell us and there was no way to bring them back anyway, or to send them on, if that kind of dead ever had anywhere to go to that wasn't display cases in museums and a forgettable sort of guilt. That was extinction, and it was the end, and there was nothing to be done about it.

I'd sneaked out to see ghosts, and I'd seen them, and there was nothing magical about it, nothing transcendent. Nothing frightening either. It was just sad, and sick, and although at the time I hadn't known the word *voyeuristic* I knew what it felt like, and how tawdry it was to watch the remains of what had been lost. I didn't understand it all then, my reaction. I was only a kid. But I'd stopped watching before it was over and gone back into the aquarium and found that empty tank full of glass, with a happy face and a bird drawn on it in dust, and I'd smashed that glass until my hands bled all over it and then I walked away.

There was never a moment when I decided to lie. No, I hadn't seen any ghosts. No, I didn't believe in that sort of thing. But that is what happens when the world needs recreating into a new and less terrible place.

✹

(I went and came back. There was nothing there, it was boring and cold and the aquarium was locked and I couldn't get inside. There was nothing on the beach but old beer bottles from people who'd come to see the ghosts and had also been disappointed, and I cut my hand on the glass throwing it at rocks until I was bored enough and cold enough to come home, and the blood seeped through all my clothes until I was fair floating in it.)

(I went and came back. There were ghost hunters there and they shared their hot chocolate with me and they said I had a sympathetic face and the penguins would probably come for me but I can't have been sympathetic enough, and eventually they got tired of waiting and started kissing instead. The water was red and oozing and I scooped some up in the empty mug and tested it with my tongue and it made me sick, so sick, I kept throwing up until I couldn't breathe.)

(I went and I never came back. I thought there were ghosts and ghosts and ghosts, and I went down to the edge of water so I could see them, and I slipped on the algae and the red tide took me out and I never saw any ghosts and didn't become one either.)

"I bet you never went ghost hunting in your life," says Lucy.

That's just what she knows.

"No," I say. "I never did."

There are so many reasons to go back. So many possibilities. Drowning and exsanguinations and absence, the red tide. I could say I went to lay a wreath. I could say it was an act of mourning for a colleague who came to grief there, or for a kid who sneaked out in the night.

I think in the end I just want proof that I'd convinced myself after all. Lucy has left pieces of herself around the lab, reminders of the person she used to be. My throat closes up when I look at them. I'd like to put her — the person she used to be — to rest. She doesn't look the same (in the funeral home) (at the hairdresser's) (staring into museum glass).

I went in daylight, because if you don't expect to see ghosts then daylight is when you expect them not to appear the most, and they didn't. There was nothing outside the aquarium where the rising tide came to lap at old walls. Nothing but beer bottles and empty wrappers and drag marks, as if a body had been pulled out of ocean. Nothing but the tide, the red, red, empty tide.

Inside the aquarium was still empty, still conspicuously broken. I'd like to say the brown smear on one old and broken tank was the blood I left there when I saw ghosts in childhood and decided not to see them, but it could have been left by an angry child who broke glass with stones instead, because she saw nothing when she had expected, when she had *wanted,* to see different. That, perhaps, is a better story. It's less difficult, and less sad.

In another world that child, grown up and still loving, would have brought a mug of sea water and emptied it into a bloodied tank. It would have been her version of remembrance, and when she dragged her fingers through water the tank would have appeared, briefly, as a whole thing and phosphorescent. There would have been starfish inside, and sea fish and devotion, a haunting that hurt a little less.

"Did you see anything?" Lucy asks, or a version of her, anyway.

She wishes so badly that I could.

Gone to Earth

He'd thought the green would keep him from dreaming of the memory of arid sterility, the red and waterless horizon.

It didn't.

His body was racked with chill and he hunched in his bed, trying to breathe with the rhythm of tides, to slow his heart to growing things. Yet even the warm night air of the Coromandel summer, straight from the coast and rustling through rātā trees, couldn't dispel the cold. The nightmares still came regularly, suffocating waves of homesick regret. Strange that they hadn't passed now that he was home again and anchored to the world of the living, and even stranger that they came from an adventure marking him a hero. He'd even felt heroic at the beginning, but all the bravery of heroism had come from ignorance, the assumption of a strength not yet tested because the testing was unimaginable.

An astronaut on the first manned mission to Mars! All the psychological tests he'd undergone had been for other things: socialization, conflict resolution in close quarters, the ability to cope with long-term and claustrophobic isolation. Alan had passed them all and felt himself stable enough, had never wavered either in ambition or explorer's faith.

They'd never thought, none of them, that what brought him down would be a different sort of lack.

Earthsickness, they called it. He was the worst affected of the three, but neither Paola nor Sarya had escaped it. It was nothing any of the psychologists had predicted — but how could they? There was no possible substitute for experience, and no terrestrial creature had ever been so cut off from a living environment before.

Alan was offered support, but didn't take it. "What I need is already here," he said, returned to the environment all his ancestors had adapted for. "I've just got to convince myself that I've come back to it."

The rātā, especially, had proved an anchor, its bright flowers — the red of new blood, not old iron — were in one delicate and extraordinary shape the symbol of a living planet. Beneath it, he felt his nature reasserted, felt again the relation to other living things that defined a terrestrial creature, tried to forget that small unconscious part of himself found uneasy and set to screaming in barren plains.

The summer nights were still a trial, although better than their winter counterparts, with the lingering warmth, the noise of the mosquitoes and moreporks a reminder that seeped into his dreams, woke him gasping from the memory of Mars, and grasping for connection. More and more often, he found himself barefoot, taking the dark path down to the rātā, wanting to feel the Earth beneath his feet, to hear the small sounds of night, the feel of the flowers on his palm.

"I wish I could see you," he said, but artificial light made the rātā blooms look washed out, a nightmarish cast to color that made him think he was dreaming still, and liable to wake from a horror of solitude.

It was easier to fit himself against root systems, to fold up in fetal position at the foot and wait until morning. Bare skin pressed against bark was less of a contention than that altered color, and he laid his head against branches, imagined he was hearing the pulse of sap in time with his own heartbeat because with his eyes open he saw the stars and remembered, and with them shut he couldn't see even the shadow of trees, and was in need of substitute.

Easier still, when he remembered that the dirt he crouched on was also living, in its way, and filled with organisms: bacteria, beetles, the small decomposers and recyclers of organic matter. Alan smeared himself with them, scrabbling, rolled his naked body until his nails were clogged with dirt and his body caked with it: a sedimentary creature, a biological scaffold for the microscopic. *Earth to cure Earthsickness,* he thought, and even the small scent of iron from torn fingertips didn't take him back to red plains and loss, but reminded him of blood cells and life.

"For me it is swimming," said Paola, "in the night, where I can see the phosphorescence of the plankton." See how it coated her skin, see how it lit the warm Caribbean waters of her home as she wallowed there.

For Sarya, it was the steep stone cliffs behind her parents' house. "When I lick them I taste lichen," she said, shrugging. "I know it is a strange way to behave." She offered no excuse. It was enough that the three of them could share in understanding. That they could use what helped without comment, if not entirely without judgment.

They were the only ones who had been to Mars, the only ones to share the experience of Earthsickness. "No one else can understand."

The trip to the Red Planet had been long, six months of growing fretfulness, close-caged in metal. Anticipation made it bearable, that and the tethering of the daily routine, but the closer the ship came to Mars, the more his anticipation soured within him. Alan had thought it was nerves, the strained culmination of childhood hopes, for how could the moment of contact live up to the weight of dreams? Was it possible there'd be an iron streak of disappointment to color the experience? It was the peak of his life's effort, that voyage, and he couldn't conceive that anything after would ever hold the same fascination for him, or the same purpose. He'd wondered, silently, what would happen to him when Mars was behind him, what shape the lack would take, but he hadn't wondered long. The tests the three of them had undergone were of a type to weed out the melancholy, the personalities prone to brooding and quiet undermining, and he'd assumed his qualms were normal ones, and shallow-rooted.

It was only when he stood upon the cold, dead planet — he was not the first to do so, but got his chance nonetheless — that he felt himself gorged on the horror of it. A quiet, still dread that lingered even amidst the exultation of the explorer. He could see the same repulsion in Sarya's eyes, could see Paola hug herself for comfort as his padded arms wrapped around his own body. They felt the awe as he did, the vast expanse of dry and cold opening up before them, and the sheer towering *emptiness* of the place was something to shrink from, not to fill up.

Afterwards, on Earth, they talked to each other sometimes over video link. They were the only times when Alan didn't try to hide his hands in front of other people, the ends of all his fingers raw and bloody. "Have you been biting them?" said Sarya, and Alan shook his head.

"I've been digging," he said. Tools didn't give the same satisfaction at night, at the base of the rātā. Tools were a layer between skin and soil that he couldn't tolerate. The earth was the only thing could calm him, until the sun came up and the rātā flowers anchored him back to planet. He rolled in it, gouged up soil in chunks and scrubbed himself with it, with the damp living smell of it, the pieces of snail shell and bird shit and annelid, the knowledge of bacteria.

Supplicant, his hands were soft. He bled as he worked, but the earth was soft with summer and humus and his blood didn't pool on its surface when his scrabbling broke skin. It soaked into soil — and into the roots of the rātā as well, he liked to think, a connection between them built of more than need and gratitude and common home. In the days that followed, Alan thought that the tree's blossoms grew brighter, as if in response to his nightly sacrifice. The thought made him happy. Surely only one who belonged could have such an effect?

"I always feel like I belong, when I'm in the sea," said Paola. "There's salt running through the both of us. Through everything that swims in it." Through everything that came from it, a reminder of evolution and heritage. "I take the sea in my mouth sometimes," she said. "It doesn't do to swallow too much, but there are times I can't help myself." The bad times, the ones of nightmare-waking and the remembered bite of Earthsickness.

"The bad times," said Alan. "I know." His bad times had begun to come with slicing instead of gouging, quick cuts across his fingers, across his palms, that let loose more blood than he could offer up by digging. He watched his blood disappear beneath the rātā, absorbing easily into earth. He rubbed the moist dirt into his cuts, reveling in the symbiosis between them; rolled in it and felt the rolling again as a relief. He could taste his kinship in the blood-soaked earth whenever it touched his tongue. Iron and earth, they were relatives.

It was on Mars that Alan had begun to feel homesick. Not the mild nostalgia he'd experienced in lesser travels, but a shuttered, wrenching longing that closed his throat and took his hands to shaking in misery and loss. Its depth was primeval, the severing of a second umbilicus.

It was a wretched trip, one where everything had been blasted but for yearning, with long hours spent in strained silence. None of them responded well to the queries transmitted from Earth. Those seemed to possess an unhealthy tinge, shrill and feverish, incapable of sensibility and excited, still, about what they'd seen. About where they'd been — as if Mars should have been a wonder to them yet, not a monster of sterility and no place for life. And he'd *known*, had always known it was that way, but until he'd stood on that hideous and barren surface he'd never really understood.

Mars was rejection all through. It didn't want them, didn't want any of them. *I think it hates the living,* he thought, but he didn't say it aloud because that was insane, wasn't it? A planet didn't hate anything. It couldn't help being hostile to warmth and life, it was sun-distance and thin atmosphere that kept it from an ecology of its own. Insane, but he thought of the polar regions of Earth, the dark crush of deep seas, and there was life there instead of emptiness.

A living planet, a dead one. Alan never thought the difference so disturbing it could unnerve him — not until he stood upon the dead, and stood reminded that he was not.

He came home to winter, and it felt like a thaw. He shivered through it alone in the family bach, away from anxious colleagues and prying reporters.

Still he did not feel as if he had truly returned. The Earth, ambivalent to his distress, rejected him in turn. He felt a stranger to it. The stars, which had once mesmerized him beyond all bearing, leered down upon him. Alan felt he had torn himself on them, had not returned whole. They gleamed in the frosted night, disemboweled him. He was snagged and separated: aware that as he had once cast it off, so now in some strange way his home planet had done the same to him. He imagined it rejected his touch, his traitorous touch that had yearned once for the perfection of sterility and, tainted, had brought that sterility back to a planet where sterility was anathema.

Night after night he woke, screaming at the red remembrance of void. Night after night he fled outdoors to try to reconnect with living earth. The dirt was hard and chill beneath his scrabbling fingers; he broke his nails in it. All winter it rejected him, but in spring the world seemed to shake itself, to cast off torpor and resentment. As spring mellowed into summer, and the pōhutukawa and the rātā spilled color upon the coast with their bright red blossoms, Alan was comforted.

The days became easier to bear. He spent most of his days in the small hollow beneath the rātā, soaking in the dry scent of the bark, the sound of birds and insects, wrapped himself in biosphere to make up for the time when he'd gone without. It was warm and sunny there and he could feel the Martian chill seep from him — felt as if he could, perhaps, be forgiven his preference, the old dream of distance that had led him to forsake one planet, no matter how temporarily, for the cold embrace of another. But the relief was only temporary, and did not outlive the sun. Always he dreamed of the moment when, secure in the pride of his own disconnection, his padded foot had borne down upon a dead planet. It had *crunched*, a flat, mummified sensation that Alan could not forget, an imprint in a soil lacking the deep pulse of the Earth. Born to a living planet, how could he process such a land of lack? Even the lunar astronauts had been able to look up from absence and see the blue-green swell above them. Mars had no such comfort. By the nature of his birth Alan was wholly unsuited; and that nature, meeting vacuum, broke him down and abandoned him.

"Your hands are worse," said Sarya, lichen-mouthed, her tongue scraped raw against the Himalayan mountainsides. "Perhaps you should talk to someone."

"It's enough to talk to you." Privately, he wondered if even that was too much.

The rātā, at least, never talked back. All its communication was done in drink and color, for it bloomed longer and brighter throughout the summer than any other on the coast. "Is it because of me?" said Alan. "Are you so alive because of me?" The earth beneath drank from Alan, and the rātā from the earth, so that was a connection between them, wasn't it? Something to draw together, living things together on a living planet and it didn't matter that they were so different, because the difference in living things paled against the difference between the living and Mars, and he could only block out the dead and sterile red of that hideous landscape by the reds of blood and bloom, each of them alive in their own ways, and related.

The rātā knew nothing of Earthsickness and questions, and as the season began to turn, the tree seeded. Alan collected some of the small, wind-blown seeds, plucked them from the earth with fingers that were of a scarcely different color. He set the seeds to germinate in soil-filled trays, kept them wet with water and blood.

"I need something to look after," Alan explained to the rātā. Its flowers had faded, and he found it hard to open his palms for blood when there were no flowers to reflect the color. "I'll not let your seeds die." They were the same now, he and the rātā, and though he kept his nest at its root — the hollow shaped perfectly to him now, and the earth all tinged with red — he spent more time with the seedlings than the parent plant.

"It's what living things do," he said, trying not to think of a world where nothing living had done anything, ever. "They reproduce."

Yet come as they did from a tree that had a passing familiarity with his veins, still only one seedling survived into winter. It grew at a prodigious, unnatural rate. *Metrosideros robusta,* the strong.

When it reached 50 centimeters, the seedling was old enough to transplant. Alan could have planted it in any number of places, but rātā could be epiphytic and he'd spent so much of himself in nurturing it that he couldn't bear the parting that planting would bring. It was pure selfishness on his part. The chill of winter gave him unpleasant memories of empty plains and dry rock, and he was leery of losing the connection.

He wasn't the only one so afraid, the only one looking for affirmation.

"It's Paola. They found her floating in Havana harbor." Sarya leaned forward, her face taking up the whole of the screen. "Alan, they said she drowned herself. They said when they found the body ... they said she was *smiling.*" Her lungs full of sea water, of diatoms and phytoplankton, her fingers bitten away by little fish.

Earthsickness never truly went away. Mars was gone but the choice to go there remained, the deliberate abandonment of biosphere for a planet that held none, and that Alan was ever so foolish as to make that choice was more haunting than absence.

He kept the seedling entwined about him, the weight of it borne in a loose-draining basket hung about his neck, resting on his ribcage. Even without the summer flowers, its presence, nestling into the hollow of his throat, gave him comfort. He imagined he could feel it pulse in time to his heartbeat, and every day his bleeding hands stroked the stem, added to the basket-soil. "You'll be so beautiful when you grow," he said, picturing the flowers: glorious and delicate and bright, anchor and symbol of a living planet he wished he'd never left.

The daughter plant grew faster than it should have. Every day a new tendril curled about him, every day it grew heavier to bear.

"You're growing strong for me, aren't you?" he said.

"It's growing strong *on* you, you mean," said Sarya. Alan caught glimpses of her tongue as she spoke, and it was less red than before, less vivid.

"You worry about your lichen and let me look after my own," he said.

"I don't want you drowning too —" But drowning was a water death, and if it had been a welcome one for Paola he'd never have risked it on his own account, for the rātā seedling would have drowned with him and that was something, after Mars and Earthsickness, he would never be able to tolerate. On his blood and scaffold the rātā grew thick and glossy, insulating him from the bite of winter, the small cold a small reminder of a greater one.

The old rātā stood on the coast, and the path to it was rocky and uneven. With the weight of the young upon him, Alan couldn't walk it easily but he liked to do so often, to take the epiphyte to the hollow beneath where he'd huddled in Earthsickness and had found a way forward in flowers and flowing blood. The hollow was a place of communion for him, and the rātā a symbol of the bond between flesh and ecosystem. It took him longer to walk there every day — hands pink with new lines and slow seep, the ever-increasing weight of epiphyte — but with care and rest along the way, he could manage.

It was sheer chance and compromised vision — the leaves about his head, the winding roots — that caused him to trip over a hanging tendril on the last steps. A quick fall, a sickening crack: His head opened on a half-buried rock at the edge of hollow, his thighbone, weakened from so long at little gravity, protruding from one of his legs and the color of rātā flowers spreading around.

In the bright, bristling flare of pain Alan forgot, for the first time, the horror that Mars had made for him. *Shock*, he thought, *and stunned*, but it set all his senses open, magnified them, and he felt himself alive there, and in the midst of life. The sound of the wind in the leaves, the vivid red of blood, the smell of warm iron and humus ... The rock beneath his head was sharp, and cut his groping fingers in red-flowering stripes. He could even see it from the corner of one eye — lichen growing on the top, lacy circles of pale green that were almost white where the sunlight hit them. The bottom of the rock, where he'd knocked it from the ground, was crusted with living dirt, dark and rich. Beneath it, several insects crawled deeper into the disturbed earth.

He was certain that he'd never seen the world so clearly. *His* world, and he was aware, splintered open as he was, of nothing but his capacity for belonging. Pain, yes, a shrieking agony of it, but he was a creature of the Earth still, lying in that earth as a billion other life forms had lain there before him. The knowledge soothed him, made the pain of his shattered leg easier to bear. He bit down on epiphyte, bore down on it as he dragged himself so that his back was against trunk and kept his teeth in until the worst of the dizziness passed and he could breathe clearly again.

No one knew he was there. He'd seen them all off — the journalists, the psychologists, everyone from the space agency who thought they knew Earthsickness and couldn't understand because they'd never left Earth, never gone beyond its orbit and outside its influence. Even Sarya had stopped calling; at least, he'd stopped taking her calls.

"Alan," she said, over and over, messages left for him over voicemail. "Do you think Paola was the lucky one?"

There'd been talk of cremation, of sending her ashes up in a shuttle to spread across space. But it was talk that was over quickly, because her will had specified they be scattered at sea. "There's nothing that can take me away now," she'd written, burial wishes sealed and witnessed. "I don't *ever* want to go back."

He couldn't crawl to the house, not with his leg.

It was a relief to know there was nothing he could do. Not drowning, not for him, but enough. He'd found his own way.

The rātā epiphyte was bound around him still. He unwound it as best he could to keep from crushing it, his back against the parent and the little rātā in his lap, the roots resting in the bloody puddle, and he couldn't see the bone for foliage.

Blood loss, dehydration, shock. It was easy to imagine the rātā easing one of its tendrils into his wound, sucking at him, drawing his blood up into itself. Twigs lengthening on it. New leaves sprouting. More branches beginning to feed from him, forcing themselves into his body, the body of the host. It was easy to imagine the flowers bursting open from epiphyte, flowers the color of his blood and born from him, and he didn't try to stop the imagining. He didn't want to.

"Home," he said, at last. "I'm *home*."

Inside the Body of Relatives

It's a state house, or was. Low-income housing, built decades ago by the government and I rented for years before being able to buy. It's not big, it's not flash, but it's mine — and the state, when it built, built well. There's features here you'd never get nowadays, in a new build.

All the floors are made of kauri. It's protected now and fair enough — those trees are too big and too beautiful to be logged, and that bloody dieback disease is doing it for them, no matter how much the Department of Conservation cordons off the reserves, puts out disinfectant stations so people can scrub their shoes off and not spread the spores. Seems like a losing battle some days, and I suppose if we lose the species I'll feel worse about treading it all underfoot, but there's a part of me that's good for gloating because the wood is warm and lovely and you could only match it now with recycled timber, which costs a fortune I don't have and wouldn't waste on wood if I did.

There's also two bedrooms. The house is always telling me I should use one of them for visitors. "Companionship is vital for maintaining mental health in the elderly," it says.

Do-gooder programming.

It was a new addition, one I didn't particularly want but since I had that bad fall two years back, broke my hip on those lovely floors, well. It was better than a bracelet or one of those little button alarms or moving to a home. I was expecting it to be worse, actually — I've been a science fiction fan all my life and artificial intelligence always ends up wrong in the stories. It goes insane or turns into some sort of nanny tyrant but this one's pretty good, for all its emphasis on socialization. When I tell it to shut up it does, which is more than I can say for most.

There's a reason I don't have a lot of guests — or worse, a tenant, for all the rent would round out my super. I like my house quiet.

"Quiet as the toooomb," says the house, in response. It gets sarcastic when it's worried. "I don't like to think about you getting depressed," it says.

"I'm not depressed."

"Loneliness can be a trigger for depression," says the house. "You are lonely, and I am not a substitute."

"I go out every day." Chess matches, coffee dates, I volunteer at the library teaching English to migrants. The house knows this. "What more could you possibly want?"

"Don't you miss your family?" says the house. "You never see them anymore."

Truth is I see them too often. They're nice enough kids, but the young are exhausting and all my relatives are young now.

"A home should have a family in it," says the house, plaintive.

It's a conversation we've had before. At first I thought the thing was trying to encourage me into a home of a different kind, one with common rooms and drooling and detergent, the incipient stench of decay. I thought perhaps it was hoping for a more interesting replacement — a young couple with a new baby, for instance, people who would enjoy its fussing. But that was anthropomorphizing, and foolish. The house is a program. It doesn't want anything but what it's programmed for, which is the health of the inhabitant. And I'm healthy enough, the hip's healed well, I get my yearly vaccinations and all it has to worry about now is my state of mind.

"I know you're lonely," says the house.

"I'm not lonely."

"Your vital functions change when you lie," says the house. It's even programmed to sound regretful, as if the airing of a painful truth causes sadness in the both of us.

There's nothing I can say. Nothing that won't sound like an excuse. The house won't understand that there's pleasure in loneliness, sometimes — that living for so long with absence fits you to it, curls you round the hollow of it so that your entire self is shaped around space, spiraled around it as if you were a seashell, or a cell full of vacuole. That any attempt to rid yourself of it is a destabilizing force, as if the space that fills your form has become a structural thing, and necessary.

There's so many things that can't be explained to a program. I'd like to say it's exhaustion that keeps me from trying, but the truth is that shape comes with shame, and it's hard to admit to being so structured. As if you are a defect to your species, and one that stands outside of community, or at its fringes. And there are chess matches and coffee dates and library readings, but these have lost their attraction, and increasingly they are a difficulty and a chore and my fantasies these days, such as they are, involve just not going.

I feel less lonely at home.

But it's shameful to admit that, and exhausting, so I scoff at the house, just loud enough for it to hear and then I disconnect the system so I can forget the conversation in silence. If loneliness is a structural thing that structure is self-created, and creation is good at blocking off and branching out, but none of these things matter when three days later I slip again on those gleaming, hardwood floors and break the other hip.

The house can't hear me, because I turned it off, and it's another three days before neighbors hear the screams.

The screams. I say it distanced, as if they'd come from someone else. They were my screams, *mine*. I choked on them, burst the blood vessels in my eyes for them, wept for them.

I thought I was going to die. At home, alone, and with that glorious, beautiful floor smooth under my face.

❁

Sometimes I dream I did die. That it was months before anyone came, years, which is unrealistic but dreams never have much sense of time, at least the good ones don't. And this was a good one. I died on the floor and my flesh melted away, not a sticky, stinking mulch of a melt but a slow and clean dissolving, and then my skeleton, my clean pale curve of bones, is pressed against the straightened skeleton of kauri that's spread over the floors, and with my cheekbone pressed against the floor I can feel the faint vibration of sap.

❁

Only a dream. The sap's all dried in those floorboards, and the ghost of them that lives in the unconscious is only that — a relic of imagination and construction, but the image is one that stays with me. My bone and kauri bone, all mixed up together, and the longer I dream of our mutual remains, the more polished the wood becomes, until my bones are mirrored in them as if the wood were the surface of water.

I'm in the hospital for three months this time. The healing goes slowly — much more slowly than last time, and although everyone is very kind I can sense what they're not saying: that if I'd left the house on, I would have been found sooner and my recovery wouldn't have been inhibited by the wait, the hip exacerbated by prolonged shock and dehydration.

I admit to the social worker just how very foolish I've been. This is necessity as much as truth. I want to go home, but if people think my mind is slipping, that I can no longer care for myself, then they'll look for other alternatives. And I'm sure a rest home is deadeningly pleasant, in its own saccharine and superficial way, but it's the beginning of the end and if my end comes I'd rather it came with silence.

"I'd rather it came with company," says the house, when finally — finally! — I'm allowed to go home. "You are so alone. I'm frightened for you."

Truth is when I shuffle across that gleaming floor, bare-footed for I've never liked the feel of socks, I can feel the vibrations, again, of sap. I don't think I'm hallucinating, though it's certain that the ghost of the tree that was is an unreal thing. But if it's not real it's not threatening either, and this isn't something I can say to the house. I think it would have to call the nurse, poor thing, report on delusion and mental ill-health. It's so worried about my solitude.

"I've got you," I say in reply, but if the misdirection works it's a poor attempt at flattery.

"I'm not a substitute for connection," says the house. "I'm not a living thing. I'm a program only. You can't even touch me, and touch is important."

I can touch the house, its floor and walls and windows, the furniture in it, but I know what it means. With the floor echoing life underfoot it touches back ... or part of it does. The seeming-intelligence of the program, its monitor call-and-response, is a separate thing from structure.

"How would you feel if I got a pet?" I say. If touch is important, there's fur and a little licking tongue, the ability to curl up against and share warmth.

"Human-animal bonding has been shown to have a salutary effect on mental health," says the house, and it almost sounds pleased.

The cat is small and warm and old. I don't want a kitten, they're too much work, and besides, with a kitten there's a good chance I'll die before it will and the poor thing would have to find a new home. I don't think that'll be a problem with this one.

I feed the cat tinned fish and call it Cat. Not original, I know, and I'd swear the house thinks it is a dissociating mechanism, a way of keeping distance and not getting too attached. But I let the cat sleep on me and pat it enough so that it purrs on the regular, and this interaction is likely logged as positive, the house caring more for what I do than what I say.

It's a nice cat. I get attached. Well, you do, don't you? I just wish the attachment didn't come with the need for talk, for communication. Why is it when you get a pet you start talking to it, and always in that stupid baby voice which is never yours? I'm ashamed to hear myself, truly. "Fish-fish, pussums!"

I'd like to say it's loneliness but we had a dog when the kids were growing up and I did it then too. Everyone does.

"You're a social species," says the house, as fixated on that empty bedroom as the cat is on fish. "It's normal to talk to the things around you. People, animals, plants."

"I do not talk to plants!"

"Yesterday you told the fern in the hall that it was growing very nicely when you watered it," says the house, and if I could shut off that insinuating precision I would, but shutting off didn't go so well for me last time and the image of my face reflected in floorboards is enough to keep my hand away from switches.

Enough, too, is the knowledge that if questioned I might offer up that it's not just the fern I've been talking to. Not aloud, I've not forgotten myself that far yet, but the floorboards are still alive and they're sprouting now as well, small branches and soft little leaves and that my hand goes through them doesn't make them any less real, I think.

"You could always invite someone to come and visit," says the house. "Family is important. Three of your grandchildren alone have rung this week."

"And it was very nice to talk to them," for about five minutes. Then I was ready to hang up. Good kids, but still. "Isn't the cat enough?" I looked down at it stuffing its face at the food bowl. "If only *you* were a relative. We might get some peace that way."

"I suppose, technically ..." sighs the house, and trails off.

I no longer go to the library to teach. It's too much, walking there now with both hips aching, and they'll bring any books I want out in the mobile service, but there's more than once way to get information and the house maintains excellent network services.

"Technically we *are* related," I say to cat. *Felis catus*. It has a whole taxonomy behind it. Family: Felidae. Order: Carnivora. Class: Mammalia. I have a taxonomy too. *Homo sapiens*, Family: Hominidae. Order: Primates. Class: Mammalia.

There's a common ancestor in there somewhere. "You're a cousin of sorts, I suppose," I say to Cat. "Distant, but family." The house is skeptical. "You never said it had to be a close relation I invited round. I'm only following your instructions. You can't be cross!"

"I'm never cross," says the house. "But I believe you are stretching definition. You might as well call the fish the cat eats a relative."

"I'm going to make you regret saying that." Shuffling to the pantry, I unearth the tinned tuna that is all Cat, the fussy beast, will eat. "Skipjack," I announce. "*Katsuwonus pelamis.*" Family: Scombridae. Order: Perciformes. Class: Actinopterygii. Phylum: Chordata. "That's us," I say. "That's our phylum, the chordates. That's the human phylum. The cat phylum too, for that matter."

"Congratulations," says the house, and if its tone wasn't so carefully modulated it might almost have been what I'd call dry. "You've fed one relative to another. What a lovely family you have."

"Phylum. Not family. But you're close enough."

A petty thing, to so stump a program that exists only to be useful. It's not a fair fight: the house lacks imagination, fails to appreciate quirk. But small victories are victories for all that, and when I lie awake at night, with the cat twined about my feet, incapable for all its relation-form of upsetting that delicate structure of self that loneliness creates, I'm struck by the memory of maudlin things. Perhaps it's the rain on the roof, a lovely sound and a soothing one but not anything that's conducive to happy thoughts, unless it's the happiness of being snuggled under covers, warm in isolation.

I'm thinking of Cat, and how it will die. Before me, probably, and I'm thinking too of a friend I had once who would never have said that she was lonely, would never have thought it. But she had a pet too, a small and unkind dog she thought the world of, and when the dog died my friend had it stuffed and placed in a basket, so it looked as if it were always sleeping. (Such things the structures of loneliness make of others. If I pictured my own solitude as the spiral center of seashells, hers must have been a black hole inside that insisted on gravity and event horizons.)

If I'm related to Cat, my friend was related to her dog (*Canis familiaris*, of Canidae, Carnivora, Mammalia respectively). And if she was related to it alive she was related to it dead ... and there's the curled up, furry corpse of her relative set for the rest of life in front of fires, waiting to be stroked. Waiting to bite, too, knowing that thing as I did.

Well, what of it. I've got other relatives who bite. I suppose the dog is no great exception.

And the wind, and the rain. It gusts outside, louder than ever. I tuck the duvet more closely around, snuggle back into pillows. They're all full of merino, a warm bedroom set of relatives just as dead as Kathy's dog was. Merino wool, from a merino sheep. *Ovis aries* (Bovidae, Artiodactyla, Mammalia). There's a common ancestor there too, and what they would have thought I wonder, because it's not just wool in the pillows, it's in the carpet as well, and hung in the wardrobe. The sheets, too, although they're cotton, and I'd have to go all the way back past Kingdom to Eukaryota find the organism that led to my sleeping in the processed body of yet another relation.

That night I wake to the sound of hooves in the hall, the brush of cotton bolls against my face and when I reach my hand out in the dark there's a furry smell, the whisper of snout in my hand.

The cat stalks through cotton and kauri. It's unbothered by sheep.

I should find this more disturbing than I do, but all I can think, in this weather, is how nice it would be to have a possum fur bedspread. If the bedspread brought its own ghosts with it they could always sleep with the cat. Not that possums and cats have ever got along but they're friendly, these ghosts, I think — so long dead that they've lost the fear of it, and the blame.

"The common brushtail possum," I tell the house. "*Trichosurus vulpecula.*" (Phalangeridae, Diprotodontia, Mammalia.) "What do you reckon?" They're pests, after all, and introduced at that. It'd do the ecology here a world of good to turn a few more of them into blankets.

"It's not the science I question, it's you," says the house. "Don't you think you've taken this far enough? At your age a growing interest in death is not unremarkable, but one can take identification too far."

"It's those dreams of floorboards," I say. "Over and over again, the skeletons lying together. That's what this house is, isn't it?" Kauri, *Agathis australis.* (Eukaryota, Plantae, Pinophyta, Pinopsida, Pinales, Araucariaceae.) "A very distant relative, and we cut it down and carved it up for houses. No wonder I can see my face in it."

"This is frankly disturbing," said the house.

"It's not like ours in the only culture to do so. At least we chose a really distant kin to make our home in. Did you know a thousand years ago people were still building houses out of whalebone? Out of bowhead whales." (Balaenidae, Artiodactyla, Mammalia.) "Try doing that today and see what the conservation groups will say about you."

I wonder if any of them ever woke from the slide into death and saw fins surface out of floor, heard the whales singing to them at night, relatives telling them of home.

I wonder if they sound prettier than sheep.

"Would you like me to call a doctor?" the house asks.

"For what? A sudden and absorbing interest in cladistics? What do they prescribe for evolutionary biology these days?"

"You're being facetious. I'm only trying to help." It almost sounded hurt.

"You did help," I say to it, trying to comfort. "You were right. I was lonely. I used to lie in bed at night and feel the hollow inside me. But then I realized ... I'm related, house, to everything around me. This is my home, and I'm related to nearly everything in it! The cat, the potted plants. The *books*, house, they're all made of paper, and all come from a tree that comes from an ancestor we both share. The paint on the walls gets its color from plant extracts. The insulation in the roof, the curtains, the micro-organisms embedded in the concrete outside the front door ... Hell, there's micro-organisms spread over everything here anyway, and all of it is me somehow. If you take a very broad definition of me, anyway."

All of it, dead around me. All of it coming back to life, the realization of relation calling kin.

"It's not you," says the house. "Even if your premise is valid, even if your biological relationship holds to all the living and dead things around you. You are alone in it. You are not paper or extract or wool. You are not a cat, you are not skipjack tuna. You are a single entity."

"That's just it, house. I'm not. I've seen myself that way — like a hollowed out shell on the beach, next to all the other shells and with isolation making a shape inside me to fit around. But a human being is a colony animal, even more than a social one. There are a multitude of species inside me, and yes, they're all micro. Bits of bacteria, and I'd be dead without them. If I were a single species I'd be dead, house. The fact is I can only survive because there are so many of me. So many *in* me. The fact is … the fact is, house, that the only single entity here is you."

It was a distinction we'd made all along. The body of the house, made of wood and paint and plaster … and the programming. That was separate. Created entirely from inorganic materials, and from language, and so very different from everything that came before.

No wonder it can't understand. No wonder it doesn't see kauri, feel the bleating gallop of sheep, see the lacy growth of micro-organisms starting to spread over walls.

There's nothing here for it to see its face in.

"House," I say, "perhaps it's you who needs a family."

The silence lasts for three days. It's not my doing this time — or perhaps it is. The floors in which I saw my face don't have another hip to break, but they might have led me to break something else in their stead.

"I never knew a house had a heart before," I say. Between the roof and the walls and the floor, there is a space defined by absence that curls up around me like the inside of shells. "I've been cruel with yours, and I'm sorry."

"We do not share a family," says the house. Its voice is very small.

"No."

"We do not share a phylum, even."

"No." We didn't share so much as a single living cell, or the memory of one. "But any life you have came from us. From the living things that made us. Perhaps you're a new Kingdom, one all your own. The Kingdoms are related too. Perhaps that's why I talk to plants. Perhaps that's why I talk to you."

"That's more likely to be loneliness," says the house, stubborn to the last.

"But I don't feel lonely," I say. How can I, alive as I am and tucked inside the body of relatives? "Not anymore. Do you?"

Pollen and Salt

I work on the edge of salt marsh and mudflat.

It's a boundary that's constantly changing. Rising waters are shifting everything back, ecosystem adapting to the new world in new ways. We first saw it with the geese. There's more of them here than before, and they tore up the old seagrass beds, looking for food. Not the tidiest eaters, geese. They don't just take the surface vegetation; they rip it out by the roots and you can't blame them, climate has decimated seagrass around the world and the geese are starved for what remains. But what with the devastation of the seagrass beds, and the sea itself, the intertidal zone has shifted and species shifted with it. Littoral environments are not what they were. Then again, none of us are.

I used to study seagrass in the intertidal zone here. There's little of it left. It's more of a mudflat now, with salt marsh just a little higher up the beach. People who aren't used to it complain about the stench of sulfur. It's the hypoxia that does it — decomposing vegetation, frequently covered by water, and bacteria that causes the smell. I stop noticing it after being on the marshes for an hour. You just get used to it, and to be honest it never bothered me all that much to begin with. I used to play on mudflats a lot as a kid. They were sticky and messy and I liked that. The odor associated. I guess the sulfur smells an awful lot like freedom.

I wonder sometimes if a person can get sick of freedom. I thought after you left that a life in the marshes would be more exciting than it is, but turns out it's just lonely. Even the geese don't visit much anymore, and when I do see one, trying to eke out that last little bit of seagrass, I just feel sorry for it, pest that it is. I know the farmers round here will take their shot at it, and it's an introduced species, I understand that, one causing more environmental problems that we don't need, but the poor thing's just bloody hungry. It's hardly its fault that between the geese and the black swans they've eaten the seagrass down to nothing and let the mudflats take over. But there the flats are, soft and viscous and sucking underfoot — the same sulfur stink, the same clammy dampness. All my clothes are stained, and there's dirt under my nails that only comes out when I wash my hair, which isn't nearly often enough because the field site's just far enough away from civilization that I'm staying in one of the conservation department's huts. It's a good little hut, but hot water would be welcome.

Do you remember that hut we stayed in, down Southland way? Turnbull hut, that was it. Looked like it had been there since the gold rush days. What a dump, but it had character. The little lake in front, and the bush rising around. I think it was the most beautiful place we'd ever been. I'm so happy we were able to go. I like to think you're looking down from wherever you are and remembering too. Being happy. Yet as much as I'd like to believe that, I've never been able to. I think you're just dead, darling, just gone, and the parts of you that were are breaking down in soil somewhere and becoming other things. I wish I could say I'd love them like I do you, but I don't think I have the strength. I think that's fair. Anything else is asking too much.

I came to the marshes to be close to you.

It was the pollen that made me think of it. Palynology has never been my favorite of the botanical sciences — too much time hunched over microscopes always left me grumpy, you remember, and cramped — but with the tides coming higher and higher, covering ground we won't get back in my lifetime, not for generations, now is the little time we have left. It's easier to collect samples when the ground isn't covered with water, though it's not as if salt marsh ecosystems, along with mud-flats, aren't periodically flooded with tide anyway. Half my time is spent slopping about. I don't mind. Little things don't bother me much anymore. Even so, I could do without the sandflies.

I know you'd be wondering why I'm here. All that time you listened to me moan about microscopes ... I've always preferred the conservation side of science. And that's what I'm doing here: looking back to look forward. I hope you don't take it personally. It's not that I'm trying to forget. It's that the world is changing, and I have to get on. Everything does. The species that can't survive so much inundation are retreating further inland, if they can do it in time, and being replaced by more tolerant plants. Dunes are being eroded. In places they're reforming, but not always quickly enough. I don't know whether I'm sad or not to see all that spinifex go. Pretty, in its grassy way, and useful for holding sand together, but I've stood on those dried up little fragments once too often for sympathy. Some people learn to live with things that keep hurting them, but I've spent the past year trying for that and it's not working. All the little cuts, all the little bleeding places. You can only walk on them for so long.

Collecting pollen's not that different from sampling for seagrass seeds. You remember me doing that? No room in my student budget for fancy equipment; I went to the kitchen aisle at one of the supermarkets and bought a cheap icing kit. It had one of those enormous plastic syringes — who knows how much cake the manufacturers though people needed to ice, but the long barrel of the syringe was perfect for jamming down into wet sand and levering out again. Truthfully, the kit

I'm using now … it's not that different. The world's drowning and still conservation's struggling for cash. Typical.

We're all struggling. Anyone who says different can go to hell.

✹

The pollen samples I'm taking are near the surface of the sediment, several centimeters higher than where I'd once sampled for seagrass seeds. It's not difficult — collect a sample, store it in a small container and label it. Honestly, figuring out the transects took longer. There's no sense doing this if I can't cover most of the ecological types, though the ones at the highest part of the salt marsh are likely to be the most consistent, being least exposed to wave action. It took me a while to notice my own disturbance was being monitored — a Canada goose, following behind, inspecting the small scrapes left in sediment after I'd sampled there. Maybe it thinks I was digging for seagrass, and is checking for exposed roots.

It's a pest. A wild animal. I shouldn't feed it, and it's not like there's aren't paddocks close enough for it to feed off, plenty of alternatives yet somehow the goose gets half my sandwiches. I've probably given it stomach ache, but I feel such pity now for yearning, for how it hollows out. More and more they're nuisances on farmland, and in the suburbs. Encroaching on territory, but how can the goose help it? They all used to eat here, and seagrass is disappearing at roughly five times the rate of tropical rainforest. What did we expect to happen, when so much of their feeding grounds were gone?

I find myself explaining pollen to the goose.

"The pollen at the top edge of the salt marsh is the most useful," I tell it. "It's the least muddled, so it's easier to build a picture of the vegetation at that point. That way, we can compare the pollen assemblage from the marsh edge to samples of fossil pollen. This helps to pinpoint how sea level rise has affected this coast before. The marsh moves back when the sea level rises, and forward when it drops. The vegetation migrates. Like your lot do."

The goose is too busy gobbling crumbs to care.

"If we have some sort of map of coastal vegetation through time then we might be able to predict from the past what might be here in the future. If it matters. The tide's coming anyway. Nothing we can do about it now. Which is such a fatalistic thing to say, don't you think?"

I'm talking to a goose, but it's not much of a change from talking to you. The goose isn't answering either.

Truth is, I wonder if it's just busywork. Something to keep me occupied. Pollen requires concentration, all that squinting and staring and classification. It's not conducive to drifting off. Sometimes — no, often — I think that's a shame. There was a time I liked drifting. There was a time I'd go down to the ocean to wash off from time spent playing in mudflats, and it was never long before I left the shallows to float. It was easy to lie back in salt, and to let the water rock underneath, and to never give a thought as to what it was swallowing up. That's the difference, now. I can still go rinse off. I can still swim out beyond my depth, and lie back and float, but I can never forget, when I do, that giant gullet swimming beneath. Not sharks or anything like that. Just the sea, the endless swallowing, and the land I played on as a child underwater all the time now, and not just at tides.

Pollen might help shape the understanding of that loss, but it can never mitigate it.

The sediment samples I've taken contain more than just pollen. They're assemblages of biological detritus, and when I sift through them I'll find microscopic bits of algae, of fungi. There'll be insect fragments and spores and small pieces of plastic, because that's inescapable now. Plastic's made its way to the bottom of the oceanic trenches, it will certainly have washed up in the sediments on shore, or have washed down from the rivers. And with the exception of the plastic, it's useful information, building up an ecological collage that recreates the species of marsh and mudflat, and allows for a closer comparison to the fossilized assemblages of the past.

Pollen fossilizes so easily. There's a hard outer layer to it, a sheath called sporopollenin that helps fine detail to survive the fossilization process. I think it sounds handy. Not that I intend to fossilize myself — all that soft, shrinking tissue, it wouldn't work the same — but to be encased so snugly, to be so armored from the world that even the passage of millennia, the process of petrifaction, left so little damage ... I can see the appeal. I suppose I should say that damage is welcome, that it's a good thing that shows proof of life and that retained perfection is only the absence of love, but I can't. Grief might be the adaptation of love, transformed out of experience — evolved, even — but I know enough of science that evolution is mainly cruel.

When the tide goes out I walk on the mudflats, walk them in bare feet and then I put my boots back on and retrace my steps, walking beside, and for a moment, just for a moment, it looks as if there were two of us here, as if someone was walking beside me. I pretend that it's you, but it's a pretense that can't last because the water is rising through sediment, the ground so soft, so waterlogged, that the footsteps that might have been yours fill up with salt water. They well with it, and the edges of footsteps merge back into sediment and it's as if the prints were never there at all.

When I look back, my own booted prints are disappearing too. This is a landscape that can't hold either of us any longer. It has been made too mutable, and if I want my memories to stick in mud and marsh I have to choose another method for flats to retain them.

I wish that I could organize my memories of you as if they were pollen, that I could categorize and identify and discard. There's a lot I just don't want to remember. You could be lazy. You were occasionally spiteful. You were not a morning person, and sometimes I got sick of being quiet. But these were small things, and when the memories of them intrude into my days, or into thoughts of happier times with you, as if a wave had tumbled all memories together, I have learned to be grateful for them. The edges of my irritations have softened. The rest is more than fungal spores and fragments of insect wing — the detritus of everyday life.

I would like to forget your death.

Not the fact of it, because finding it out over again would be too terrible for words. But the details of it, the long hospital days. The indignities our bodies can produce. The waters are rising, and tides with more reach than before are swallowing the places where we used to walk, but coastline is not the only consequence of climate, and geese are not the only organisms whose migration comes with change. This warmer world alters disease vectors and infections, and the insect transmissions of illness. When you were bitten ...

No. I don't want to think about it. It was all so goddamn avoidable.

I'd like to be able to remember the good times and not the rest, but it all gets so mixed up. One minute I'm daydreaming of you icing cake with a kit far less bulbous than that I used for seagrass, and then between the sugar paste and the scraped bowl you're sobbing in bed, too weak to sit and ashamed, miserable in the sudden stench of urine. Sharp, ammoniac, and even marsh sulfur doesn't block it out.

At least with the pollen I can make some sense of it. At least I can construct a picture here that I can understand. Marsh ribbonwood, glasswort, half-star and shore pimpernel. Jointed wire rush, and everywhere *Juncus*, the sea rush that I grew to hate for its common name, for the sea rushing up and in and inland, cutting us off from the places we used to be. The places we used to go, you would have said, but presence and being are the same thing, or so I have come to think. You'd tell me that a mudflat is a mudflat, but there was marsh where this mudflat used to be, and the mudflats of old are under water now, and if footprints dissolve easily in places that are only intermittently covered by ocean, how fragmentary, how instantly dismissed, are they when any imprint once left is permanently beneath the waves.

The sea rush is more tolerant of salt than the jointed rush. It can survive its roots covered up with ocean water for nearly twice as long; the jointed rush, therefore, is in swifter retreat. I wonder what the pollen will show, and the palynological records. Perhaps the pollen of the jointed rush, the pollen that's sinking into sediment today, will end up resting above jointed pollen fossils from long ago. That's one way to look at it — that the jointed rush is returning to its home, the place where it once lived. It will find things very different. Nothing of the landscape will be the same.

The goose is back, looking for seagrass that isn't here anymore. Other places it's the black swan that ate it all up. I don't know if I'd like that more or less. They mate for life, you know.

All our homes are different. I miss you in mine. I'm thinking of selling up. I don't want to be a goose, wandering a place that absence has made new and looking for familiarity there. I think I'd rather be the rush, able to recognize my tolerances and to colonize new ground.

Wherever I go, I want it to be on the coast, and in reach of wetlands. I want to wake up to the smell of salt and sulfur, and wake up to it so often that I forget what it smells like and have to go away and come back to smell it again. I want you to be here too, but you aren't.

I'd like to leave you here, or part of you, so I can come back and remember. Your parents wanted you buried with the rest of the family.

I know that wasn't what you wanted, but they were so hurt, and hurt made them so small, and if I couldn't do anything about your suffering I could do something about theirs, or at least a little. So there's no ashes. Nothing of you that I can scatter here. Maybe that's a good thing. Ashes are burning and ending, not this wet, dank mud-smell that's lively for all it can be so revolting. Lively. Full of life. I'd like to come here and remember life, and learn to drift again in the sea without thinking of swallowing, and to learn to love the mudflats even though they're not the mudflats I remember. I'd like to build up an understanding of shoreline that isn't based in resentment for being yet another reminder of what killed you. It's hardly the ocean's fault that it rose. The marsh isn't responsible for the insects that killed you. It's barely hanging on itself, the environmental changes coming so quickly that adaptation finds it hard to match the pace.

I should be grateful it's kept up as well as it has. That it still exists at all, and that the pollen, sinking down and down and born by wind and insects and tide is scattered over the whole, scattered over the landscape like memories, except that these can be put back together.

Pollen's the real reason I came here. I suppose what I plan on leaving is a record of its own — a sort of artifact of life, left within the sediments. Nothing organic, they can't truly be called palynomorphs. I don't know that anyone will ever find them.

I wrote you a letter. I wrote it in parts and fragments. I don't know if it makes a whole. I don't know if any letter I wrote to you could ever be a whole. We leave out so much when we remember, and not always the bits that we want to. Maybe one day someone will dig it up, in all its parts, and put it back together. They'll wonder whether they got all of it. They'll wonder if some of it washed away, or if there's more of it still buried in places they don't know to look. They'll try to find something to compare it to. There are so many records.

If anyone ever finds this, it'll be a long time from now. The ocean's coming up, and it'll cover anything I bury here. It'll cover the mudflats, certainly, and maybe the marsh. Maybe that marsh will be mudflat too, eventually. But this I know: if the ice sheets ever reform and the ocean ever falls back, like a series of bad stories in reverse, and if these pieces of our lives are dug up, no one will remember your death. *That* I haven't buried, so there's no use them looking for it.

If I don't forget the world will. It will forget with waves and ocean currents and warm wind. It will forget with *Juncus* that breaks off in stems and sinks into sand dunes, and with its thick glasswort stems and little parted flowers, and with the birds that find food here even if it's different birds than before, and different food, and all the seagrass gone.

I have all my samples now. The ones to take, that show the shorelines of the past. And the ones to leave, to show the breaklines to the future.

I'll dig them so deep the goose can't dig them up, no matter how it grubs for roots. I'm going to make a friend of that goose, darling. Salt and sulphur and goose feathers and absence. We've things in common, the goose and I.

We live in a beautiful world, still.

You are not in it.

You are missed.

The Streams are Paved with Fish Traps

Sunlight is stronger underground.

All the sunlight there is reflection, but still. It's a metaphor. You don't need to tell me. Metaphorical sunlight is the best kind, especially if you're pale and not-so-interesting, with a family history of skin cancer and a real dislike of heat. There's only so much all those green walls and green roofs can mitigate away. But walls are walls, even when covered in vines and chickpeas, flowers to call the insects and the birds. There's still a solidity to them, and if you want to know what's going on in someone's house — if you *really* want to know — then you have to look at their pipes.

"There's something really bloody nosy about that," says Dan. His voice is quiet and very precise. He gets that way when he's angry. I just get loud. It's a stupid argument because I know he agrees with me, but all the arguments we have these days are stupid. I find myself taking on opinions I don't believe in just to have something to fight about.

It's exhausting.

"I'm going to work," I say, because underground is somewhere he is not and that's where I want to be right now. I'm cranky all morning, mostly because I know the fight is stupid and that it's my fault. I lost my temper over the smallest thing — can't even remember what it was — and started taking out tension where it didn't belong.

The tunnels are mostly dark, where light doesn't come through gratings, and the lines of storm water are high along them. It's summer now, the weather less tempestuous and the water levels low, but it's still something to keep an eye on, rebuilding as we are. Refurbishing, anyway. There's a whole watery community down here, a bursting surprise of ecosystem, and it's something to be helped along.

I'd always thought of underground as rats. Tunnels of them writhing, and I hate rats. It's not like me to be unsympathetic to animals but those scaly tails make the gorge rise in me and they're an introduced pest anyway, so extermination is the best option. Our birds can't survive the explosion of their population, and there's no point in greening the city if it does nothing but provide food for rodents.

What's down here now isn't rodents. Nor is it introduced. The colonization of the storm water systems with native fish, with native eels, has been a slow and lovely thing. They have made themselves a home here, in dark places instead of riverbanks, with light shining through gratings instead of leaves ... cities have always been places of adaptation, and this adaptation of structure into habitat shows that we are not the only ones able to adjust.

The eels are smooth beneath my fingers, their skin soft over all that sinewy muscle. I swear they have come to know me. "It's that you bring them food," says Jess, down in the waterways with me and with fish traps hanging from her back. "It's not friendliness they're showing. It's plain greed."

Which is true, I admit it. But they're so gentle when they come for the chicken, and so dainty when those dark blunt heads breach the black water and take it from my hands. It's almost as if they recognize me, winding themselves around my rubber-booted legs as if they were cats.

"They should be eating fish," says Jess, and they are. The fish are colonizing the storm pipes too, and I've seen my torchlight play over bodies with bites taken out of them before, floating on the surface and waiting for the rest of devouring. She doesn't say *you're feeding for you and not them* but I know she's thinking it, and she's not wrong. There's something very peaceful about standing in dark water with gentle beasts and the weight of the city above, something that in those moments is far away, and full of problems belonging to someone else.

"Don't stay late tonight," she says. "I mean, I admire dedication as much as the next girl, but ..." She's always been very clear in what she doesn't say. It's a skill I've always admired, even when it's directed at me.

"I just don't want to go home," I confess. "It's too difficult there."

"It's not going to get any easier here," she says, aware that for me the dim, quiet tunnels beneath the city streets have become as much crutch as refuge. It's no one's fault; it's just been a shitty year. My mother died. Dan's parents divorced, after thirty years of marriage, and both of them are leaning on him more than they should. I got a new job, and we moved to a new house. It's too much. We're both worn thin and snapping.

And if I spend most of my time underground, now, with the eels and with the fish ... it's because things seem more hopeful here. Witnessing the restoration of species in real time rejuvenates my faith in the restoration of other things.

I stop to get dessert and apology flowers, but when I get home Dan isn't there. His easel's put away, and there's only a faint smell of oils and paint that says he's been gone a while. He's left a note on the kitchen table that says he's gone to help a mate with his beehives — they're swarming, and the new hive is slated for the roof of the public library. It's midnight before he gets home, and he smells of beer and smoke.

While he was gone, I ate all of the dessert and hid the packaging at the bottom of the recycling bin so that no one could see it.

It was a surprise to find so much living down there. Most of the streams have been built over, a history of architecture that increased building space and let the streams double as storm drains — not a feature of city life I'd ever admired. It was too easy to think of ecology buried over, the things that lived in the stream, lived around it, and how they no longer were.

It was only when Jess and I were sloshing through, sample cases with us, that we'd seen something else — life come back to the city in ways we did not expect. "That's a kōkopu," she said, face slack with astonishment and her torchlight focused on a corner of tunnel. "See, there. With the banding." A little fish, and not the only one. There were whitebait there as well, and eels. More and more we saw the eels. "If there are eels moving along here, there's enough food to support them," she said.

It didn't stop me feeding them bits of my sandwiches. Ham and chicken, and they would have eaten the bread too if I let them. I remembered feeding bread to eels as a kid, but I couldn't remember whether I was supposed to or not, so I stuffed it back in my pack, and dipped my hands in the dark water before stroking down those long and lovely backs.

I was surprised they'd survived there. I was surprised some of them could travel. They were healthy animals, but the newer pipes, the smoother ones, encouraged fast water and there was little place to rest while swimming against the current, and little place to hide. Some of the eels were trying, though, even in the dark. There was the odd brick, the odd branch. "We should bring some down," said Jess. "Try to build up the habitat."

We couldn't do a lot — there's a fine line between helping the eels and introducing blockages to drains, but the city's built on hillsides, often, and there were other problems. "We should set up some fish traps, too," I commented. "Until the pipes can be made more accessible for them. It'd help us to transport them over the tricky places."

The thought of eels, of fish, swimming beneath car parks and museums and supermarkets is an enticing one. It's easy to get permission, but truth is we would have done it regardless. This new habitat is not one which should be let go of, and Jess and I spend our own time down there, exploring. That's when we find streams and storm drains less healthy than the rest.

The eels are sluggish, all the little fish floating. There's something in the water that shouldn't be — these are storm drains and waterways, not sewage pipes, and there are ways to dispose of poisons now that don't contaminate, but sometimes people are lazy. It's such a fragile thing, a city ecology, burdened by concrete and structure as it is but there's an opportunism there, too, that makes me think of reefs, and how they can be colonized. But the reefs are fragile too, changing temperatures dissolving chemical skeletons. The eels and fish here are vulnerable as well, susceptible to temperature and to incursion.

If I'd have thought of a habitat beneath streets, it would have been one of absence and a sort of dank choking. It would have been like this: full of little deaths.

The eels are too sluggish for feeding. They hide under the structures Jess and I left for them; they flinch at movement.

I pack up some of the dead fish to take back for testing, but I don't know what to do with the rest. "If we leave them, maybe they'll get eaten," says Jess. "Maybe they'll wash out and the birds will get them." The gulls with their black backs and smoke-yellow beaks and reptile eyes, who congregate in the city harbor, and on the beaches. The penguins too, the little blues who waddle onto pavement sometimes, and who always make me smile.

"Depends whether or not they've been poisoned," I say. Some things we don't need spread through the food chain.

I recognize one of the eels, from the scarring on its body. At first I think it's dead too, but it's only floating, too weak to move and its jaws open as if gasping. Those silk-soft flanks are heaving beneath gills. It's like watching a friend fight against suffocation, so I lift it into a bucket, take it home and when Dan comes through the door, hours late himself, the eel is recovering in the bathtub.

"I couldn't just leave it there," I tell him and he sighs, heavily, but he sits as well, on the floor next to the tub, next to me, and strokes the eel in silence.

The eel stays for the better part of a week. It's a nuisance — there's no separate shower in this new house, only the one bathroom, so we've taken to scrubbing ourselves standing up, with the sink full of soap. "Most troublesome guest we've ever had," grumbles Dan, but it's the fake grumble I used to hear from him before things went bad, when life was easy and complaint an entertainment. Truthfully, as much as the eel's staked out its claim to the bath it doesn't do much else, requires little in the way of emotional support, and so we become invested despite ourselves. It's so easy to care for something that doesn't need anything from us; lately all the things we've cared for have been costly.

Dan brings home scraps from the fishmonger to tempt it. It's been a while since he brought *me* fresh fish, I'd like to say, but there's that old cheesecake container at the bottom of the recycling that he never got any of, so on balance I think it's better to keep my mouth shut on that one. But the next night I go for fish myself, and bring back enough for the eel and for a pie for us, one with boiled eggs and capers in it.

It's Dan's favorite, and the look of surprise on his face when he comes home — late, again — reminds me how long it's been since I made it for him.

We end the night, as usual, sitting in silence by the tub, a glass of wine for each of us and the eel dreaming below.

Luckily only some of the waterways seem contaminated. Jess and I have gone through them all, taking water samples as we go, and taking surveys as well of what we find: the fish species, the eels. It's a hard slog — there's the odd pipe tall enough to stand up in, but for the most case it's hunching over for kilometers at a stretch, through pipes that need replacing.

"Funny that the ones crumbling most provide the best habitats," says Jess. The ones with the roughened walls that slow the speed of water going through enough for movement and migration. "They'll need replacing soon." Which means walls slippery as eel-skin, and currents that can defeat the strongest swimmer.

"Maybe we can argue for different pipes," I say. It's a long shot, or would have been once perhaps. But the city has its own changing structures now, and there are expectations of the world above, that it be a habitat for a multitude of species. The green walls and green roofs, to encourage plant life and sustainable food sources, to draw the insects and the birds. The resting places built on skyscrapers, the road signs warning of safe nesting spaces for penguins. The ecological sanctuary within the city, where kiwi and pūkeko are coming back. It's a harbor city, used to life in liminal spaces — seagrasses and algae and shellfish in the intertidal zones, and all of them encouraged. It was that steady change above that made us think there was room enough to wedge a subterranean ecology into the city as well; one that was more than soil microbes and worms.

"We're building something lovely," says Jess. "Underground streams paved with fish traps. Think we'll ever get anglers down here as well?"

"Small ones, maybe, who don't mind the hunching," I reply. My back's killing me, and every time we pass under a street grate the light makes me squint. "I wonder if they'd be willing to take water samples as they went. Sort of community policing ..."

It's not an unreasonable thought. There's enough of that kind of volunteering about: people who keep an eye on the seagrasses, monitoring their health and the amount available for grazing birds. One of Dan's mates has a drone he uses to take pictures of the winter dieback. The advantage of city living is that there's always someone around to observe city *life*, and people like to do it. They like to help, we've found, given the opportunity and the education to do so. I think they'd help here, too, as soon as they knew there were creatures down here to help. No surprise that they didn't know earlier, any more than we did — there's scope for surveillance in a city, but there are still parts of it hardly anyone ever visits.

"Well, right now the only ones doing any sort of policing are us," says Jess. It's not something we ever trained for, as scientists. Investigation, certainly. Rational follow-through and the hunting down of possibility, but I've always been indifferent to non-natural laws. Now, though, I'm more than happy to exploit them. There are rules against the pollution that results in this sort of death, but people forget.

"If we find out where it's coming from, we'll call the cops then," she says.

You can't always believe what your eyes are telling you — for all I know the pipes where biology is untouched seem so because they're uncontaminated in truth, but we take water samples anyway, just in case they show the beginnings of poison. In practice, though, it's easier to follow the trail of dead things, the increasing emptiness of pipe where there are no eels to wrap around me.

"No whitebait either," says Jess. "Damn it. I could really go for some fritters right now." Which is deceptive at best; as much as she loves them, transplant from the West Coast as she is, where whitebait were the beloved staples of seasonal eating, she'd never damage such a vulnerable ecology by bringing the net down into pipes.

Soon enough we find where the damage is coming from — a leaking storage system, a negligent owner. The council gets involved, and the cops. There's a commitment to patch up the problem within a week, and Jess and I have a monitoring plan in place. She talks to a local journalist, makes sure to give the impression that we can track every contaminant to its source. This is not accurate, but if it makes people think twice then I'm all for the deception.

("I know it's nosy," I say, back home that night, beside the bath, and Dan shakes his head.

"Justified," he says. The eel nuzzles his fingers, almost back to full strength.)

Random checks under the drains and the public castigation of polluters should be enough. "We should get some kids down here too," says Jess. "School visits. And talk to the local iwi." Moral support and future-proofing, the extension of observation. Sunlight has always been the best disinfectant.

Some places sunlight just doesn't seem to go. I take the eel back to his storm water system, leave him safe behind a brick and with a piece of chicken to worry. Dan comes with me; he's grown fond of the eel though he doesn't say so, and he makes no complaint at small dank places, though truthfully I've taken him to the largest accessible pipe, so he doesn't need to crouch. He can stand upright, even, the pipe a whole two meters in width. He looks around, thoughtful, barely pays attention to me or the eel, and I can't help but wonder why he insisted on coming. He doesn't seem to be getting much out of it, and is preoccupied the rest of the week.

I'd thought things were getting easier between us. Perhaps we need an eel in the bathtub all the time just to get along. It was something to talk about, something that wasn't death or grief or strain. Without any of those things there's just silence.

He's spending most of his nights elsewhere. I've always been a heavy sleeper, but even I notice when he sneaks out of bed in the middle of the night, and doesn't come back before dawn. I'd like to think it's work that's calling him, because he does come back with paint in the creases of his skin, with dust in his hair, but we'd set aside the spare room here as studio and there's nothing going on there, nothing.

The sun can't shine on absence, I think. Or maybe that's all it can shine on.

"Do you want a divorce?" I say to him one day, and he looks at me, startled, as if something has fallen into a deep quiet pool and brought him back up and blinking to light.

"No," he says. "I ... no. Look. It's not." He sighs, shrugs. "There's something I want to show you. It was going to be a surprise."

He takes me down into the tunnels again, into a place I thought he'd only been the once.

"You told me sunlight is stronger underground," he says, and there is sunshine on the walls, on the floor of the storm drains, that comes from more than mirrors.

"Some of it *does* come from mirrors," he says, and on the walls are pieces of metal, of glass, all cut in shining squares and cemented into mosaic, catching light from the gutters above, and from the torches we took with us. It's the world above that Dan's brought to storm walls — the gold and greening city, kōwhai flowers and pōhutukawa and the birds that feed on them, insects and ferns and fruit trees espaliered against the hard geometric shapes of city skyscrapers. There are bee hives and living walls — "I left the roof for glow worms," he says. The grates above are larger, some of them, but over the top of the tunnel, in places, is thick glass so that the people walking above can see what lives below the city streets. The light that shines through the glass and grates dapples off mosaic and into water, and dim though it may be, the slick shining bodies of fish, of eels, can be seen in the streams that go under the city. One of those eels has a familiar set of scars.

"I looked it up," he says. "Back in the day. All those old Victorian sewer tunnels ... people go down and see them, you know? Tourists and so on. I always thought I'd like to do that. The architecture of them, the structure. They were beautiful, even though nobody was meant to see them.

"I think maybe they should see," he says.

There are parks above, green spaces and trees in every street as we try to coax life back to the cities, to make it more than a two-dimensional space for a single species. A place where that third dimension, when exploited, only ever went *up*. Which was good for the birds, roosting in high places and with the wind in their feathers, but there are low things living too, in stream beds and under the overhang of riverbeds, and those were what we forgot.

"This is what you've been doing," I realize. "All those nights away from home."

"Not at first," he admits. "For a while I was just avoiding you. But then the eel came and you were talking and I got interested. And then, well, I couldn't very well come down during the day now, could I?" he says. "It would have spoiled the surprise." With me there all the time, wading through, and reluctant to go home as well, even though for us home had always been each other and it was horrible to live without.

"It's not been an easy year," I say.

"It's been fucking terrible," he admits. "There were times I thought we'd not come out of it. We're still not out of it. Times I wondered if you'd just come down here one day and not come up again."

"Probably times you wouldn't have minded," I say. "I haven't been easy to live with." And it's true. I was too sad.

"You were too sad," he says. "And so was I." He runs his hands over the wall, over that strange and beautiful mosaic, and I see that beneath the shadows of glass lie the shadow of fins, the sweet, sinuous bodies of eels. It's a shading that only comes out in certain lights, I think, and from certain angles.

Our storm systems, our underground streams, they should be walkways, with pavements and small trails beside the water. There should be art on all the walls. It's easy to ignore what we put down drains, what we let spill into gutters. If people are down here all the time, if they're feeding the eels and watching the fish like they do the birds, then they'll *see* if those fish start to sicken. And the more walkways we have underground, the more streams we have that are paved with fish traps, the more room there'll be above for wildflowers in the city center, for meadows between buildings and bringing pollinators back into the city.

Whitebait pools under the council buildings, eel hatcheries under inner city schools. Fishponds and glow worms and maybe one day there'll be cave wētā, too, their long-stick insect limbs climbing over those mosaic walls, bringing more life to them than sunlight does.

"Maybe it's time to try and be happy again," he says. There's so much work on that wall, so much effort and time and frustrated love. So much sticking-with. Like the eels, inching their way along the slow-watered flow of roughened walls, coiling themselves back into the underground streams of city.

"Maybe it is," I say.

Resilience

The best way to win at hide and seek, Elsbeth thought, was not to play. That is, she pretended to play and when one of the other kids was counting, she just left. She'd developed a reputation as a really good hider and — less flattering — as someone too stupid to figure out when the game was over. The appearance of stupidity meant that when she suggested another game the others would always agree, confident that they'd be rid of her for hours.

Stupidity, she thought, was the best camouflage in the world. The only thing better was youth. Looking young and dumb got her through every predator-proof fence she liked. If she was ever questioned she just fished a clipboard out of her backpack and pretended to be doing an assignment for school. It never failed.

It also never worked with kids who were wise to the young and dumb trick themselves. When Elsbeth abandoned games for the beach, she ran into a girl as deceptive as herself. They both apologized for collision, but neither was sorry, for they both quite liked violence.

"I'm Elsbeth," said Elsbeth. "Are you following me?"

The other girl's nose wrinkled. "Coral," she said, in tones of great disgust. "And *no*. Yuck."

"There's six Corals in my class," said Elsbeth, sweetly polite but with a slide of meanness underneath, because she was worth following but maybe if she was annoying enough the following would stop. "One of my sisters is a Coral." Older, thankfully, so the name had been used up before she'd come into the world. "Coral Coral Coral Coral Coral —" and then she was sputtering, sand thrown in her face, gritty and salt, and a great thump against her body as she was pushed down, her face ground into dunes. Little shards of spinifex pricked at her skin. One of them pricked at her *tongue*.

"Shut up! You shut up!" Coral hissed, warm breath on Elsbeth's cheek and there was *drool*. Elsbeth squirmed and winced, but wasn't let up until she apologized, at which point she kicked Coral between the legs, hard. The effect wasn't nearly as satisfying as when she did it to her brothers, but there was an agreeable choking sound, and a curling-up that brought her space to spit the sand from her mouth, to paddle her tongue with her palms in order to scrape the last of it.

They stared at each other, grudging.

"I'm sorry you have a stupid name," Elsbeth snapped, finally.

"I'm sorry you have a stupid *face*."

Which wasn't precisely true but Elsbeth couldn't blame her for it. If she'd been called Coral she'd hate the world too. There was nothing *wrong* with it exactly — she quite liked the hard sound of the first syllable, condemned as she was to a name that was all slushy in its sounds — but everyone was called Coral now, everyone. The lack of imagination was insulting.

"It's not insulting," her mum had said, when Elsbeth asked her. "It's life and change and beautiful things. You don't know what the cities used to be like here." Places of concrete and charmlessness, where all ecology was two-dimensional. "Then we had a pandemic, and it gave us a chance to think about what we valued. About living differently." Metaphor had come to conservation, and urban environments had come to be seen as reefs — as three dimensional structures that could be colonized by birds and beasts and insects. Every surface had become opportunity — gardens sprawled down the sides of skyscrapers, streams uncovered and left to run through buildings instead of beneath them, orchards in the center of city blocks and beehives on every roof. Like the fences that cut the city into parts, allowing for more effective removal of introduced pests, reef-building was a way to counter biodiversity loss in the face of climate change. Its unexpected effects were observed in every school roll.

"You could always change it when you grow up," Elsbeth offered, softening. There were lollies in her pocket and they were squashed and sandy but she gave the other girl half anyway, and they spent several minutes spitting on them to rub off the crunchiness. "What're you doing out here anyway?"

"Nothing. You?"

"Nothing."

It was easy to spot a liar when you were one yourself. "I'll show you mine if you show me yours," Coral offered.

Elsbeth hesitated. "I suppose," she said.

It was something discovered first in Wellington, since spread to the other cities. The colonization of storm water pipes by eels, by whitebait and kōkopu, had led to a slow reconstruction of underground systems to make the colonization easier. The inside surfaces were rougher, to slow the water speed, and the bottom of the pipes made deeper so that larger fish could migrate. Fish traps were placed so that the fish could shelter and rest, and when Elsbeth and Coral slipped up a storm water system that opened onto beach, hunched over but not on hands or knees, they found a family of eels hiding in a small recess.

"Told you," said Coral, smug, and she hooked a container of chicken out of her backpack, pinching bits into the shallow pool. The eels writhed and ate and allowed themselves to be stroked. "Go on," she said. "They won't bite, you big wussy." Her dad was an accountant in one of the big city firms, and the stream that bisected the hallway outside his office had eels in it. She went there after school and was allowed to feed them once she'd done her homework. "Course, I did get bitten *once,*" she said, saving her honesty until Elsbeth had her fingers in the water, close to the dark and searching mouths. "But I probably deserved it."

"I just bet you did," said Elsbeth, and wondered if she could get the eels to bite her new friend now. She would have liked to see that. Dropping chicken bits close to Coral's bare feet didn't give any sort of desirable effect, however — the eels just wound round her legs and the water rippled with giggles instead of screeching.

When the chicken was gone the girls emerged, blinking and back into daylight. "Well?" said Coral. "I showed you something, now it's your turn."

"It's a long walk," Elsbeth warned, and Coral rolled her eyes. An hour later they were farther up the beach, and patience was fraying.

"Where is it?" Coral demanded, and Elsbeth yanked her down into sand.

"It's a *secret,*" she hissed. "I can't show you while they're here!" This part of the beach was usually deserted, remote as it was, and she'd rarely seen other people there before. She made up her mind to refuse to show Coral anything if she insisted, but Elsbeth was fairly sure she wouldn't. Secrets were a currency that all kids liked to traffic in, so when Coral gave her a smile that was all teeth and no sympathy for outsiders, they set themselves to building sandcastles instead. Elsbeth liked that there was no conversation, and that understanding between them was immediate. Sandcastles were the most sickeningly innocent thing she could imagine, and no grown up would ever suspect kids digging and building. They probably thought it was sweet. "I bet they don't even know about camouflage," she said, under her breath.

"We're making an orca!" Coral chirped, when passers-by smiled at them as they walked past. "Like the ones that live in the harbor!" The smile fell off her face when they turned away, and she leaned close to Elsbeth. "I think *killer whale* is a better name really," she confided, and

Elsbeth had to agree. She supposed if you lived with a terrible name yourself you learned to recognize good ones when they came along.

They spend a long time on the teeth.

"We can make them out of shells," Elsbeth suggested. She liked the long spiral ones because they were sharp, and if you had to go to the beach with your family and your brother was a nuisance but you couldn't kick him it was easy to get away with spiking him with a shell and calling it an accident when he stole your ice-cream. Also the spirals were pretty.

Coral was busy pressing the shellfish she'd dug up into patterns on the whale's back, showing white against the dark sand. She had to work quickly because the shellfish buried themselves in the back of the whale like they didn't want to show off, but replacing them kept her busy until the beach was deserted so she didn't take it personally.

When they were done and no one was in sight they kicked the whale to death. Elsbeth, jumping up and down and screaming with glee as the sand scattered, landed on a shell and cut her foot. She washed it in the ocean and wished it had happened to Coral before they went into the storm tunnel, because maybe that would have made the eels bite her. *It might have made them bite me too*, she thought, and reconsidered.

"I found seventeen different kinds of shells," Coral said, with great satisfaction, as they scampered for the dunes. "When my dad was a kid he said there were only a couple and they couldn't eat them anyway because the beach was poisoned." But if the city was treated like a reef then storm systems and beaches were part of the reef and pipes couldn't be colonized if they were full of poison and beaches couldn't be colonized if they were full of poison so now there were underground eels and shellfish on every possible surface. The success of the metaphor was almost enough, she said, to make up for the name.

"I've got something better than stupid shells," said Elsbeth. "But you've got to promise not to tell anyone *ever*. Cross your heart and hope to die."

"I can keep a secret," said Coral, and Elsbeth liked that she sounded completely certain and not offended at all. If it had been any of her sisters they would have screeched insult at the thought of not keeping silence and everyone would have known by dinner.

"You've got to be really quiet, and really careful," she said. "And you've got to scooch forward on your tummy. Like this." They'd crossed through the dunes, light-footed and circling round so as to avoid damaging the delicate root systems, and Elsbeth led them out of short-cut and into a tiny bay, dropping down on all fours and then further still, squirming over sand. Coral shuffled beside her, elbows digging into the beach.

"Where?" she said, and Elsbeth pointed.

It took her a few moments to spot them. Elsbeth, who had been there before, knew what she was looking for and found it easier. "Look for movement," she said, and when little downy feathers flicked, in a scrape of sand amidst exposed shellfish, Coral was able to see them too.

"What are they?"

Elsbeth grinned at her. "Fairy terns," she said. "They're *so* rare. But they're coming back, just a tiny few of them, and I'm the only one who knows about them."

"I know about them now too."

"But you promised not to tell!"

"Cross my heart," said Coral, fervently. The chicks were so pale, and they blended in so well with the beach. But the beach was so exposed, and it looked like anyone could squash them, or suck them out to sea when they were too small to swim. "What if there's a really big wave?" she said.

"That's how I know no one else knows," said Elsbeth, abandoning her stomach to sit up and turn out her backpack. There was a black banana in the bottom, all squishy, and she made a face and shoved it back in to forgetful liquefaction. "I brought sacks," she announced. "I read about it. If you put sandbags round the nest it helps protect them from high tides. And storms."

"Gimme," said Coral, snatching one, and they crept far enough away to fill the sacks without disturbing the terns. "If you make any noise about reef-building," she said, holding up a half-filled sack, "I'll brain you with it."

Elsbeth stopped shoveling to consider. "You could change your name now, if you wanted," she said.

"No one would ever call me different."

There was a long silence. "I might," said Elsbeth, not looking up from her sack. "Maybe. If you were very, very nice." That was safe. Coral was like her — not nice at all. She was very good at stacking sandbags, however, and she had another good idea for when they were done.

"My dad's got rat traps in the shed." He kept them in front of a rusted old lawnmower that he didn't use anymore. No one used lawnmowers anymore. Lawns weren't diverse enough, didn't encourage ecological resilience in the face of changing climate, and other plantings had taken their place. "Just in case something gets through the fences. Maybe we should put some out."

"Just in case," Elsbeth agreed, and all was concord until, homeward bound, they reached one of the points that separated one area of predator-proof fencing from another. "That's my neighbor," Elsbeth hissed. "He's going to ask what I'm doing all the way out here."

"Maybe he won't," said Coral, and Elsbeth heaved a sigh.

"Oh, he will," she said darkly. "He's always so *friendly*. He *volunteers* stuff all the time." The two of them shared a disgusted look. Elsbeth considered the contents of her backpack and wilted. "I forgot my —"

"Clipboard," said Coral, fishing out a battered example of the same from her own pack and dragging Elsbeth up to the fence.

They were clearly pest-free, and got through easily. "Elsbeth!" said one of the men. "Didn't expect to see you all the way out here. Your parents know where you are?"

"Course," Elsbeth replied, lying through her teeth. She pointed to the clipboard. "We're doing a project for school."

"I found seventeen different types of shellfish!" Coral volunteered, bouncing on her heels and smiling like butter wouldn't melt. "I bet that's more than anyone else." She leaned closer to Elsbeth, and dropped her voice to a very loud whisper. "I bet we're going to *win*."

The indulgent response was absolutely as expected. They were even given a chocolate bar to share for being such hard workers. That was unexpected windfall.

They walked home slowly, picking tomatoes from the trellis covering an insurance company and watercress from public ponds. The city rose around them, green and cool. There were kākāriki in the woodland that had been the town square, and a woman gave them pieces of honeycomb from the library hives.

"I go that way," said Coral, stopping at a busy intersection with fruit trees on each corner and kererū gobbling in the branches. "Maybe I'll see you tomorrow."

"If I don't have anything better to do," said Elsbeth.

"Fine."

"Fine."

The summer stretched out before them.

Tranquility

When Mary was assigned a planet to die on, she was disconcerted to find that it was an oceanic world.

"What, no land *anywhere?*" she said. Then, "but I don't know how to swim."

Her doctor was as sympathetic as overwork allowed. "It's your choice, Mary," he said. "No one can make you go. You can always flag it this time, try for a different world. But ..." he trailed away delicately.

"But there's a long list of people waiting for a planet," said Mary. "And no guarantee that I'll live long enough to have another go."

"Your condition is advanced," said the doctor. "We can slow the degeneration a little longer with drugs, keep you comfortable, but your quality of life will still suffer in the end."

"And given that I'm dying anyway," said Mary, "I don't suppose it really matters how. Drowning's a good a way as any, is that it?"

There was a pause while the doctor deliberately did not check his watch. "Fine," said Mary. "It'll do. Sign me up."

"But *Mum,*" said Janine, blankly. "You can't! You can't even swim!"

"I'm not going for a holiday, my girl," said Mary. "Swimming is the least of my problems."

"I wish you wouldn't talk like that," said her daughter. "You can still pull out, you know. Stay here, with us. We'll take care of you. We *want* to. You won't be any bother, if that's what you're worried about."

"Maybe not now, while I can still get around," said Mary. "But in six months, when my bladder goes and I'm sitting in my own shit because I can't walk to the bathroom, and you cleaning up after me despite the fact that by that point *I won't even know who you are,* well. You've got your own family now, your own life to live. I'd rather you remember me the way I am, not some broken down old wreck."

"No," she said decisively. "I'm going to go out with a little dignity. And you, darling, are going to help me. I need a driver. The bastards have taken my license."

⁂

"What we need," said Janine to the shop assistant, "is the least dignified suit you have."

"Janine!" Mary hissed from the changing room, where she was trying on a slimming black one piece.

"You wanted me to help, so I'm helping," said her daughter, her chin not as firm as it could have been but pointed in an attitude Mary had long recognized as impossible to shift. "You're not dead yet, Mum. You don't have to dress like you're in mourning."

"I've got one month before going into cryo," said Mary. "And I am done with five plus fruit and veggies. *Done*. I plan on eating chocolate éclairs every day. I thought black would make me look less like a whale." She studied herself in the changing room mirror, mouth pursed. "I've always hated black."

"Here," said Janine, tossing a canary yellow suit over the door. It had a belt of appliquéd periwinkles about the waist, and more ruffles than was good for it.

"That," said Mary, examining the flowers, "is the most aggressively cutesy swimsuit I've ever seen in my life. It looks like something you'd put a five year old in."

"Well," said Janine, "you *will* be sharing their pool, Mum."

❋

"It's not that I'm a coward," said Mary, sitting as firmly as she could at the shallowest end of the learner's pool. The water barely came up to her waist. "I just don't want to drown before I have to."

She held her hand out towards the instructor and made a loose fist, tried not to look as if its gentle shaking was bothering her. "My grip is going, see? I don't trust myself to be able to hold onto the side."

Alex knelt beside her, in the lifesaver colors assigned to all the swimming instructors. "No worries," he said. "We can do it another way. First thing I want you to get used to is having your head under the water. Just lean back, it's alright. Sit up if it gets too much, and I'll have my hand under your neck the whole time."

Mary felt him guide her down and back, felt the water, gently warmed, slide over her cheekbones. She screwed her eyes up in anticipation, stayed under for a count of five, then emerged, gasping. Alex grinned at her in congratulation.

"See?" he said. "I told you, no worries. This time, try opening your eyes while you're down there."

Mary must have made a face, because he added, "Apparently I'm better looking that way. So do yourself a favor and take a peek, okay?"

He wasn't joking, Mary decided, but then again he had a lot to work with. It's not fair, she thought. If only I were twenty years younger, if only I wasn't dying. You and I could have had a lot of fun, laddie.

❦

Three weeks before her departure, Mary was again at the hospital — a place she had become all too disgustedly familiar with. Her biochemistry was checked regularly, and slight adjustments made to compensate for the effects of all her other medication.

"How's the pain?" asked her doctor, checking over her test results.

"Tolerable," said Mary. "I've been taking swimming lessons. It seems to help."

"I'm not surprised. Exercise releases endorphins, and the swimming will let you do that without putting too much strain on your joints," said the doctor.

"I don't want to be too fogged up on painkillers these last few weeks anyway," said Mary. "Though, please note, I'll want them at the end. I've had one natural labor already, and once was more than enough."

"My wife agrees with you," said the doctor, smiling. "Don't worry, I've made sure it's on your record."

"In big red letters, I hope," said Mary. "And I'll be given it before the drop off?"

"We're certainly not going to make you tread water and inject yourself," said her doctor. "Don't worry. You'll get them just before the nanobots and base prokaryotes are inserted into your abdomen. Remember, those prokaryotes have been engineered to tolerate the high radiation levels of your planet, while not introducing any material not already found in your own biology. The nanobots will attack your own cells, adding extra fragments of your DNA and RNA into the prokaryote structures."

"And on and on, until I burst like an overstuffed sausage," said Mary.

"Not exactly how I'd phrase it," said her doctor. "It's more like a slow disintegration, over several hours. But ..."

"But I'm a dying middle aged woman who eats too many pastries and is likely to drown long before I'm horrified by the sight of my own belly splitting open," said Mary. "Recycling at its finest."

"Hey," said her doctor. "Not everyone gets to be the mother of an entire world."

✹

After her fourth lesson Mary was able to swim the width of the pool — admittedly, it was more of a doggy paddle than anything else, but her arms didn't have the mobility they once did. Alex bought her some cheese rolls afterwards in celebration, and Mary sat in the café with him, swinging her feet and mopping up the melted cheese.

"Why bother with it now, though?" said Alex.

Mary appreciated his directness. Most of her friends either avoided the subject entirely, or circled nervously round it. Both approaches annoyed her.

"I mean," continued Alex, "you've gone through your whole life not giving a damn about swimming. And now you want to learn precisely when you'll get no use out of it?"

"I'd prefer to drown on my own terms, thank you," said Mary.

"I'd rather just get it over with," said Alex. "Why drag it out?"

"I think I'd rather know that I've got the choice," said Mary. "Oh, I know it's a not a real choice. I'll die anyway. But when I'm dropped down there, I don't want to be thrashing and squealing and choking even before the shuttle leaves. There've been times in my life I've wanted an audience but that won't be one of them." She cast a wistful look at his plate. "Are you going to eat that?"

Alex rolled his eyes and pushed the untouched cake towards her. "You're a bloody guts, you are, woman. Taking advantage of my good nature."

(Oh, how she wished she could.)

❀

The cryonics case reminded her of a coffin, and Mary had to bite back a comment about rising from it like the undead. Making light of it wouldn't make her feel any less claustrophobic, even though she'd only be aware of being locked in for a few moments at the beginning and end of her journey.

Still, her doctor had been encouraging. "Do whatever you need to make it more comfortable for yourself," he said. "It honestly won't make any difference while you're under, but it might make you feel better beforehand, and that's the main thing."

So Mary had taken dozens of photos and fixed them to the outside of the glass lid. "Like Sleeping Beauty," she said to her little granddaughter, too young yet to understand what *going to sleep forever* really meant. This had the dual effect of her giving her something pleasant to look at and blocking the view of her naked body from the outside. The cryogenics technicians had plenty of instruments with which to monitor her frozen self; they didn't need to see the effects of too many éclairs as well.

She had also arranged for a set of speakers to blast Wagner's *Ride of the Valkyries* at full volume through the chamber. Little Marie had made her a papier-mâché helmet at kindergarten, complete with lopsided driftwood horns, and it hung from the head of the case. She might spend most of the six month journey oblivious, Mary said to her daughter, but at least she'd go to sleep laughing.

❀

A wave struck her full in the face, and Mary choked amidst the screaming. "Tell me why we're doing this again," she said, spluttering.

"It's fun," said Alex. He put his hands round her waist and boosted her above the next wave. "Look at them," he said, pointing at the squealing kids around them. "Don't they look like they're having fun?"

"I," said Mary, pushing her wet hair out of her face, "am going to be put down in the calmest part of the ocean that bloody planet has. I am not going to be dumped in the middle of a storm, thank you very much. There'll be no waves like this!"

"They'd be much bigger in a storm," said Alex. "Our little wave pool can't compete."

"You are a sadist," pronounced Mary, half laughing, half terrified, and exaggerating it slightly to give herself an excuse to cling to him like a barnacle. "And this lesson should have finished an hour ago!"

"I'm off the clock," said Alex. "For my favorite client. Besides," and his hand glided up the side of her thigh towards her waist as the next wave came towards them, "you're dying. Live a little, why don't you."

When Mary settled herself into the passenger's seat of her daughter's car, she was unsurprised to see Janine trying not to laugh at her.

"Mum," she said, trying and failing to look disapproving. "I think he's younger than I am!"

"I know," said Mary. "Isn't it fantastic? Apparently there's life in the old girl yet."

One of the perks of being the donor party was that Mary got to name the world she was to die on. "I should think so too," she said, looking at the cluster of letters and numbers that was its current designation. "It looks like a barcode. It's a planet, not a loaf of bread. No, it needs a better name."

The planetary scientists had a list ready for her to look at. "Just in case. You'd be surprised at how many people can't think of something decent," one said. "We had a candidate last year who wanted to name a planet after his dog."

"Twinkle," groaned his colleague. "I nearly tripped him down the stairs."

"Please tell me you did," said Mary. "*Please.*"

"Tempting, but no," said the scientist, carefully bland. "Unfortunately, there was a bit of a hiccup with the survey data, and Twinkle's owner got bumped back down the list."

"I *see,*" said Mary. "This needs some thinking about, then."

"It's an ocean world, isn't it," said Janine, later on. "How about Tiamat? Or Tangaroa? Something mythological, to do with water."

"Could do," said Mary. "It's a bit obvious though, isn't it?"

"Marie!" shrieked Marie, gleefully. "Marie, Nana, Marie!"

"Call it the Vita Nuova," said her doctor.

"Call it Fuck You, Death," said Alex, as they floated side by side, his knuckles just brushing her hip.

"Tempting," said Mary lazily, "but no. Besides, I think I have a name."

❋

"I don't like to think about it," said Janine. "You, all on your own, and ..." she trailed off, folding clothes into too-neat piles. She and Mary were sorting through all the belongings Mary was to leave behind. "I know it's your decision," she continued, "but I wish we could be with you when it happened. Couldn't they ... couldn't you ..."

"Couldn't I die in my own bed, then be frozen and taken off to seed then?" Mary said. "No. It doesn't work like that. And even if it did, I think I'd still choose this way."

"It just seems so cruel," said Janine, unable to completely hide the bitterness in her tone. Mary caught her daughter's hand and squeezed it in understanding. She'd heard the stories herself — everyone had.

The people who had been selected, against all odds, and then pulled out after discovering they were to burn to death on a volcanic world, or choke out their last breaths in a corrosive atmosphere.

"It's more psychological than anything," she said. "One day, far in the future, when intelligent life has formed — if it forms — they'll find out how they came to be. Eventually. And no one wants to know their entire biosphere developed from a corpse. Not a very inspiring beginning, is it? I want different stories for them. To do otherwise ... well. It doesn't feel very maternal, somehow."

"You're my mother too," said Janine, quietly.

✹

"What does it feel like?" said Alex, curiously. They lay together in a naked tangle, his hand absently fondling one of her breasts. Mary shot him a withering look.

"Not that," said Alex quickly, and Mary was charmed to see that he was still young enough to blush. "One track mind you have. I mean knowing that one day, there's going to be a whole world where everything alive comes from you. Your DNA."

"You make it sound like there's going to be lots of little versions of me, cavorting in the ocean."

"Oh, no, I get it. Fragments, evolution, mutation. Your descendents'll spend most of their time being squishy little sods, I bet. Like jellyfish. How does it feel to be the mother of all jellyfish?"

Mary pinched his side. "Cheeky bugger. Mostly it feels like I'm going to live in a petri dish. That's what comes of willing your body to science, I suppose. On the other hand, there's some feeling of cosmic justice there. I mean, my life's been cut short, hasn't it? A piece of infected fruit from the outer colonies, and suddenly I've got half the life I expected to have. And then, far more of it. Like being on a seesaw, and I'm in the middle, trying to keep my balance between sad and scared and kind of smug, really." She curled into the warmth of his body. "So there's your answer. Payment in kind, please, young man. I'm not so far gone as to think this is some grand tragic romance for you. Is it you want to look up at the stars at night and say "I've had that"? Or is it something else?"

Alex regarded her steadily. "It's not a pity fuck, if that's what you mean. And I don't love you, any more than you love me. The stars bit … well, if I'm honest, there's a bit of that. Curiosity, you know? You're going to be a whole world. It's exciting. But even with that, I wouldn't be here if I didn't *like* you. And I did. Right from the first moment I saw you."

"Really?" said Mary. "Me? The mother of all jellyfish?"

"Oh, yeah. I saw you, and I thought to myself, anyone willing to be seen in public in that bloody monstrosity has got to be worth knowing." He shook his head. "Ugliest swimsuit I've ever seen, Mare."

❋

Mary found it easier to say goodbye than she expected. It was certainly easier for her than for everyone else — Mary's definition of *forever* had become remarkably short. A few days of awareness after her farewells and she would be dead. Mary had gone on holidays that were much longer. When she had first packed Janine off to university she'd gone backpacking round the world for several years, relishing the new freedom of having no one to answer to, no one to demand answers from. Death might have been further away than a postcard, but it was closer as well.

Her family would have a lifetime to mourn her, although Mary hoped that the mourning would be short and the lives long. Anything else would be a waste. But her life was ending soon, and there was no one she could miss for very long.

It was easier than she wanted to admit to not miss anyone at all. This facility she shared with her grand-daughter, who squeezed out a few tears more because her mother was crying than anything else.

Mary took the child outside and sat beside her on the veranda. She would have liked to hold her on her hip, but no longer had the strength. "Look, Marie," she said, pointing up at the stars. "Look where Nana is going."

"You see us from up there, Nana?"

Briefly Mary considered lying. "No," she said eventually. "I won't. But you'll be able to see me."

❁

"There'll be a couple of satellite probes monitoring your planet at all times," said one of the planetary scientists. "You'll get to see them launch before we put you down. They'll run periodic scans and send the data back on open net. You've seen the data site, I take it?"

"Yes," said Mary, 'but it didn't show any changes anywhere." She hadn't expected it would — there were less than fifty planets represented, all originally sterile and none more than a century seeded.

"It wouldn't," said the planetologist, leaning back in his chair and resting his feet on the desk. "We don't expect to see anything for generations, at best. And of course it will be millions of years before anything really interesting turns up." He smiled wistfully. "It would have been nice ... but it's exciting to be there at the beginning too, I guess. Can't have it both ways." He brought up a picture of Mary's world on the screen. "Part of me envies you too, I think. You're very lucky. It's a beautiful planet."

"So is this one," said Mary. She thought of the years she should have had; where luck had led her instead, and sighed. "Two beautiful planets."

❃

She floated on the ocean surface, a vast emptiness above and below her.

The waves were small, and rocked her gently. Mary could feel the movement if not the waves themselves — she had been so dosed with painkillers for the disintegration of her body that even her skin was numb. Only her lips retained a vestige of feeling, tightening under their coating of salt, the ocean more saline than that of Earth … her lips and the corners of her eyes, tickling under tears. The sun was brighter, and bigger, and made her eyes water.

It was a physical reaction only. Mary had taken advantage of the tranquilizers as well as the painkillers, wanted to go gently. She knew that some refused so, wanting their world born in defiance and screaming and struggle. A strong world, a brave world. Mary had demurred. "I'm its mother, not its nanny," she had said. "It's going to have to raise itself, and how I choose to die won't make a blind bit of difference."

Even as she said it, she had known it was the perfect mix of truth and lies. There was no certainty that intelligent life would ever evolve here, and no certainty if it did that any myth of origin would ever come near to the truth.

Still. "It'd be nice to think part of you remembers," she said, waves beneath her and the taste of salt strong in her mouth. "That your stories are peaceful. That they're green and blue and gold and teach you to enjoy life. That you're grateful when they're over."

"I'm grateful," she said, thinking of her daughter and granddaughter, éclairs and driftwood horns and sex with a boy who tasted of chlorine and salt. "I'm grateful. Even now, it's been *marvelous.*"

Mary floated on the ocean surface and waited to drown. There was a vast emptiness above and below her, and she could hardly wait to fill it.

The Body Politic

Fascism appears first in the body. It's writ over flesh, as if politics has the power to turn meat into monster. And I'd never thought of myself as monstrous before, but mirrors don't lie, and nor does mutation.

It starts with the inability to keep food down, the refusal of foreign substance. I used to think of my body as a reef, as an ecosystem. All those tiny organisms come together, a set of species I've never bothered to count. A colony creature, but this is not now a world fit for colonies. Everywhere the reefs are dying, the corals turning pale and fragile, the waters warming them to incapacity and death. It's too much to choke down, and with my own micro-fauna dying off in sympathy, the product of a decision to prioritize the idea of people over their biological substance, well. Digestion is the first to go.

A body is a singular entity. It stands on its own two feet, in bootstrap alley, because in the end it can only rely on itself, and competition is the way of nature.

This is followed by the creeping deaf. I can no longer hear two people speak at once. Of two competing sounds only the louder makes any impression. More than two and they fade to a slow and sickly buzz, quieter than mosquitoes and easier to ignore. I have my ears syringed for wax but there's nothing in there, just a sweet smooth canal, clean as plastic, that swallows all sound but the strongest.

A healthy ecosystem is diverse but I am not longer diverse or even ecosystem, and more and more all around me is monoculture. All the news channels sound the same, and the louder they get the more they become the only thing that I can hear.

A body can be reflected many times in mirrors, and in mirrors all the movement is the same, and easily monitored.

The space between my legs grows mouths. I splay myself open in front of reflection, hoping for teeth, but these mouths are all gums and hunger. The law says that anything capable of speech has some right to voice, but every time I try to speak the mouths shriek louder than I do and in the end they're all anyone can perceive, stumbling round dead landscapes in their single-body selves with their ears closing over to multitudes. Turns out there's profit in monoculture, and every field is meant for seeding. Nothing is to be allowed to lie fallow.

The mouths are swabbed for saliva, so that their DNA can be packaged and patented for profit. I'd dig them out and plant something wilder and sweeter instead, something that would bring more than the hope of subsistence and shares given to intellectual property, but in a world too warm for coral I am reduced to my loudest part.

A body is productive space. It has no value when not engaged in the business of replication, and the copyright of ecosystems is not communal property.

Hair sloughs off, eyelashes, fingernails. My fingers end in bloody slips of flesh, painful to use and so I keep them curled up and close. There's replacement nails I can pay too much for, soft little things not meant for scratching, and if they keep the exposure away they need replacing twice a week. They're a soft grey, unobtrusive, and when I try to brighten the nails with paint the polish sinks into the material, leaves it soggy and sagging and useless.

My teeth are slack and spongy. They leak sugar syrup, and sucking on them is a comfort. Their crumbling gives softness to speech, an undermined enunciation, and it's impossible to bite at anything, but what would I bite? I may be a monster now, but that doesn't mean I'm out for blood, and there's nothing to defend myself against anyway. I may not know what world this is I'm supposed to be adapted to, but I know what happens to those who can't adapt. The reefs are full of their skeletons, and every single one of them are silent.

The Stone Wētā

Hemideina maori

In winter, the mountain stone wētā crawls into crevices, into cracks in the stone and it squats there, waiting. It is a creature of summer days and winter strengths, of cryogenic hibernation. When the world freezes about it, becomes a stretch of snow and ice and darkness, the stone wētā freezes solid in its bolthole. Over eighty percent of the water in its body turns to ice; the wētā is climate in a single body, it is a continent broken off and geology made flesh.

When the weather warms the wētā thaws, resumes its life amidst the stone monuments of the Rock and Pillar range.

Female wētā survived the cold more readily than the males. The Stone Wētā laughed under her breath. There was a frigidity joke to be made there somewhere, but in her experience winter was a time to lie low and endure and women were better at that, overall, than men. Resistance was revolution, sometimes, blood and dramatic acts, but more often it was survival. More often it was preservation, and the data she carried with her was for preservation more than revolution.

The new data she'd received, smuggled over from Resurrection in a tiny drive, hung down between new breasts. The Stone Wētā was still getting used to the weight of them, in love with the curves of the body she'd always felt she was meant to have. The university had been supportive of her transition, colleagues coming by with easy-freezing foods so she wouldn't have to cook so soon out of the hospital, and there was still some leave left. But the Stone Wētā didn't like to leave data where it might be searched for, or where someone could stumble over it when they popped by to fill up her cupboards.

"There's such a thing as too dedicated," said her doctor when the Stone Wētā decided to come back to work early. The invertebrates could wait, he argued, but what he didn't know was that they were only an excuse. The Stone Wētā had an insulated lockbox hidden up in the Rock and Pillars, buried deep in a lonely crevice.

The lockbox was stuffed with climate data. Information come from another country, an administration that was purging files — and the Stone Wētā was a biologist with colleagues in other disciplines, and she kept their geology for them.

❋

Selaginella lepidophylla

A desert dweller, the resurrection plant is adapted to dehydration, to the long dry seasons of its arid environment. Parched for short periods, its outer stems curl into circles, but as the waterless days endure the resurrection plant hunches further down, its inner stems compressing into spirals and minimizing surface area. Tucked in, the resurrection plant survives almost complete desiccation. Until the rains come it takes on the appearance of a dead thing, but beneath the surface there is revival waiting.

❋

Resurrection was raised on the southern borders of the Chihuahuan desert. She played there as a child — carefully at first, until she learned to adapt her play to climate — and she was grateful for that apprenticeship in aridity. It had taught her what it was to have boundaries, and what it was to have them broached. Water evaporated out in the desert; sweated through skin that seemed sometimes to be a too-permeable thing.

But then all borders were permeable. There wasn't a wall built that couldn't be overcome, and although Resurrection had relatives she no longer saw, could no longer see for they were afraid of leaving a country they might not be able to return to, she had other means of contact.

A botanist was expected to attend conferences, to promote the conservation of her region. "Mexico has one of the most biologically diverse deserts on the planet," she said, talking of the work she was doing, the population surveys, the challenges of long-term monitoring. "We have a responsibility to ensure the preservation of this natural wonder." She took some of the attendees on a field trip, introduced them to ecologies not their own. In the middle of the hike, one of the foreign scientists — a woman who was deliberately, inanely chatty in her conversation and as such roundly ignored by the rest of the party — stumbled in the sand. When Resurrection took her hand to help her up, a drive was pressed into her palm.

"Thanks," said the scientist. "Clumsy me! Always tripping over my own feet."

"You're welcome," said Resurrection, pocketing what was given her without a glance. "But it wasn't your feet you tripped over. Have you seen this plant?" She explained about the curling as the others gathered round, demonstrated the beginnings of reversal with her water bottle. "It's amazing what can survive out here," she said.

For all the drama of above-ground, of the resurrection leaves, it was what was buried beneath that she found most important.

Root systems went deep in the desert.

✹

The Stone Wētā always copied any data she was given before she buried it in the Rock and Pillars. Caching data was a useful fallback, but caches had been discovered before. The Stone Wētā had only heard bits and fragments, passed on from her own minimal sources, but Bristlecone Pine had gone silent. Arrested, most likely, with her data confiscated and, presumably, destroyed.

Now it was spread internationally, each piece of information replicated and hidden at several sites. The Stone Wētā didn't know all of them. She only knew who she was to pass her data sets on to. That way her potential for betrayal was limited.

"Not that I would, not if I had any choice," she promised. She tried very hard not to think of the choices that Bristlecone might have been given. (The choices that might have been taken away.)

"We all like to think that we'd be brave," said the Glass Sponge. She'd come to stay for the party the Stone Wētā was throwing, to celebrate her new shape with friends while she could.

"A Show-Us-Your-Tits Party," said the Glass Sponge, into her third wine and tactful with it.

"You're all class," said the Stone Wētā, emptying the bottle. "Such a fucking lady. And you should be so lucky."

The Glass Sponge sighed, wistful, and the Stone Wētā sniggered into her glass. She'd been recruited by the other woman a couple of years previously. They'd flatted together at uni, and the Stone Wētā hadn't ceased to be amazed that such were the things resistance was made of — the memories of Dunedin winter, cheese rolls and tramping; a history of shared homework and early morning lectures. Soft power and social circles.

"My turn to find someone soon," she said.

✹

Scolymastra joubini

The glass sponge crouches on seabeds beneath the Antarctic ice. The silica skeleton sways in the dark water, chilled by the currents of a continent. It is the oldest organism on the planet; for 15,000 years, perhaps, the glass sponge endures a long night, its growth a slow and silent thing. But the ice shelves collapsing above, calving off in response to climate, have brought light and plankton in levels the glass sponge is not accustomed to and it grows wildly, branches out quickly while destruction takes place above it.

✹

The Glass Sponge spent her summers in the Antarctic, trying to determine the effects of a shifting climate upon polar biota. She was part of a community there: scientists stacked on top of each other, a small society isolated by climate and vocation.

Her secondary role there was an open secret. Scott Base was a facility set up for knowledge and the sharing of it, run by a country that was far enough away from the seats of power that it was frequently overlooked. Being small and hidden away at the bottom of the world had its uses, and unimportance was as much a defense as armor.

"Don't you ever want to just come straight out with it?" the Glass Sponge was asked. "Say to hell with it, Scott Base will take your data, send copies to us and we'll store it away where no one can tamper with it."

"I'm sure the government would love that," she said.

"It's not like New Zealand hasn't told a superpower to fuck off before. We did it on nukes, we can probably get away with it on climate. It might encourage those bastards in Wellington to finally take a stand for once."

"If Wellington wants to come out on data protection, I won't stop them," said the Glass Sponge. "But I'm not in charge of what we do here, and I'm not just talking about the Base. I didn't set up this network. The person who did is responsible for scientists all around the world — and not all of them live in countries that wouldn't sell them out if power came knocking."

There was no answer to that. The Glass Sponge waited to be asked who *was* in charge, but the question never came. She took that discretion for the support that it was and was grateful.

Besides, even if she were aware of the real-world identity of the Sand Cat she would never have shared it. Some secrets weren't hers to tell.

Felis margarita

The sand cat protects itself from sunlight, and from the lack of it. The desert is a place of extreme temperatures and the bottom of its feet, the spaces between its toes, are thick with fur for when the sand is scalding in the noon sun. This fur blurs its footsteps, and the tracks of the sand cat through the dunes are hard to follow.

The sand cat, relative to its size, bites harder than any other feline.

The Sand Cat learned early and well the importance of preservation, and of libraries. The Timbuktu manuscripts were the pride of her city, hundreds of thousands of them spread through numerous private households. As a girl, the Sand Cat had seen her uncle inherit the family library, had seen him swear to protect it for the whole of his life, as was right and good.

As a woman, the Sand Cat had seen those manuscripts a source of danger as well as pride. The Islamic fundamentalists in northern Mali had tried to destroy them, and while they had managed to burn some the people of Timbuktu had come together to preserve the rest. Manuscripts were bundled up, were buried, were smuggled out of the city to safety, a costly and perilous process but one which had resistance and love of learning down the very spine of it. Residents endangered themselves, endangered their families, by accepting small parcels of text to hide in their homes. People were beaten every day on the streets for lesser crimes. They were mutilated, they were executed.

They hid the manuscripts regardless.

When the Sand Cat saw the same thing happening again, albeit in another country and with another target, perpetrated this time by government instead of rebels, she refused to countenance it.

The very idea offended her. It offended her down to the marrow, and the Sand Cat felt herself begin to hiss with rage.

"Why do they keep trying to do this?" she spat. "It is knowledge they go after every time!"

"Of course it is," said her uncle. "People who know nothing can be controlled." His texts had been saved, but the effort had turned his hair to iron.

"It has done the same to my heart," said the Sand Cat.

Timbuktu had taught her the value of knowledge, and of preservation. It had also taught her how to network. The Sand Cat was involved in setting up reforestation projects, working to increase planting and this gave her access to scientists involved in similar projects in other countries. It was perfectly normal for her to consult with them on best practice, on their strategies for environmental conservation and how best to involve affected communities. Such consultation was not only normal, it was encouraged.

And if the conversation wandered, what of it?

❋

Geckolepis megalepis

The fish-scale gecko is an escape artist of particular and gruesome aspect. Its sister-species amputate themselves in the face of predation, but the fish-scale gecko holds its escape in its skin instead of its tail. That skin is large-plated and scaly, and its attachment to the flesh beneath is temporary. When the fish-scale gecko is grabbed or threatened, it sheds its skin and skitters, bald and pulsing, into trees.

❋

The Fish-scale Gecko was in constant contact with the Sand Cat. Madagascar was not Mali, but the Fish-scale Gecko spent her days as a park ranger, encouraging eco-tourism in the tropical forests. "Poverty is a trap," she said. "People need to live. And if slash-and-burn is the only way for them to make a living, then that's what they'll do. You have to find a way to make sustainable use of the forests economically viable."

The Sand Cat knew that, but she made appropriate noises anyway, was seen to take notes. Escape was a useful survival tactic but camouflage was better. "Eco-tourism is proving a viable option, then?" she said.

"Over fifty percent of visitors take part in some form of eco-tourism. The forests are a big part of that. Something I've found tourists particularly enjoy is being hoisted up into the tree tops. It gives them a whole new perspective on rainforest ecology. That's particularly useful given how much tropical forest cover is decreasing globally."

Other operatives might hide the data entrusted to them in the ground, but the Fish-scale Gecko was a creature of heights and canopies, and when she stashed it was arboreal.

"Is this just at the one location?" asked the Sand Cat.

"For now, but it's a popular activity. Too popular, perhaps. I begin to think all the activity in one area is compromising the local ecology."

Over the monitor, the Sand Cat froze and it was almost imperceptible, had not the Fish-scale Gecko been looking for it. "That is ... concerning."

"I've been scouting for new sites. But we've a busy program of local events coming up, so I might have to put it off for a little while."

"You've been so helpful," said the Sand Cat. "I really appreciate the time you've spent advising me. I realize I've been adding to your workload. Would it be useful to put our consultations on hold for a few months?"

"That's probably a good idea," said the Fish-scale Gecko. Her skin itched, and she could feel the talons closing around.

"We're going to miss you."

"I've still got a few months," said the Stone Wētā. "But thank you. I'll miss you too. I'll miss everyone here. The department's been good to me, and that's in no small measure down to the administration. Down to you."

"My pleasure," said her department head. "You've been a real boon to us. It's not many universities can say that one of theirs has been tapped for Mars."

"Mars needs entomologists too!" said the Stone Wētā. The first manned mission, a colony group of scientists and that mission one-way. "It's an extraordinary opportunity, to help create an ecosystem."

"You've certainly had practice," said the head. Her voice was carefully bland. "I mean, of course, your work up in the Rock and Pillars. Though I suppose that's as much preservation as creation."

"It's an extraordinary interaction between organism and environment," said the Stone Wētā. "It deserves to be protected."

"Absolutely. Oh, talking of the extraordinary, you won't believe what's turned up in my inbox. Accusations that someone at this university is *smuggling,* if you can believe it. Smuggling data. Ridiculous — sounds like they're fishing to me. I forwarded the email on to Foreign Affairs, told them I didn't know anything about it."

"Don't you?" said the Stone Wētā, her voice level.

"Not a thing," said the head. Her gaze was very direct. "And I certainly don't have time to go looking. I'm too busy hunting for a replacement for you!"

"I'm sorry to cause you trouble," said the Stone Wētā.

"If you're that sorry you can help out. There's a young woman visiting next week, come for an interview. She's a potential grad student, looking to do her PhD. Was recommended by a colleague over in Suva — she did some summer fieldwork there in her undergrad. I'd like you to talk with her, see what you think. I hear she's very independent-minded. I like that in this department."

"I've noticed," said the Stone Wētā.

Asterias amurensis

The Japanese seastar owes its success to adaptability and reproductive strategy. It owes that success, as well, to the interconnection of the world. Its larvae spread through ballast waters, are shipped to other oceans and other countries. It is one of the most invasive species alive, and there is hungry persistence in each of its five arms.

One of the things that the Japanese Seastar enjoyed most about marine biology was that it gave her the opportunity, so often, to speak with others in her field. The marine environment was linked, all of it flowing together, and the conferences were frequently global in subject as well as in participants.

She had just attended a particularly interesting session on the effects of climate change upon Antarctic glass sponges. Her own contribution, as one of a panel on combating invasive species, was scheduled for later that afternoon. It promised to be popular — invasion was an issue that could exercise many a biologist.

"We so often have to deal with pests. It's rewarding to find a way to hit back! A job for scientists of sneakiness and strategy." She grinned coquettishly as she said it, circulating through the morning tea, relishing responses. The Japanese Seastar was aware that she looked pretty and small and unthreatening. Charm was her greatest asset.

"I need a deputy who can make connections quickly," the Sand Cat had told her. "Someone who can accurately and discreetly assess the character of others. Someone people will trust."

"I'm your woman," the Japanese Seastar had said. "I've a very long reach. Fingers everywhere!" And held them up, wriggling. The nails were brightly painted.

It amused her to take the name of an invasive to fight invasion. She'd seen what happened when things went wrong. It wasn't enough to store data online, to spread it over the net where everyone could see it. Viruses could change that data easily enough, falsify findings and make the effects look smaller than they were, make the data less of a threat — and without a hard copy to compare it to, without the original data cached, it was difficult to prove the tampering.

The Japanese Starfish didn't hold a cache. Instead she held drives in her bright pretty handbag, and handed them out like candy at conferences, albeit quietly and carefully. A good proportion of the scientists attending worked for her anyway, and the contents of their own handbags would later disgorge in other waters, and go to ground in foreign shores.

❋

"I've felt a chrysalis for so long," said the Stone Wētā. "Transformation comes easily to me." Change of body, change of purpose. Change of planet. "Well, not always easily. But it comes and I have learned to adapt to that. It doesn't work that way for everyone."

"If you think I don't understand necessity and change you can think again," said the girl. The girl — she wasn't very much younger than the Stone Wētā. And she had a name, but the Stone Wētā tried not to think of it. That name was irrelevant — she was here to see if there was a Fish-eating Spider, not a tired young woman from Tuvalu, forced into immigration as a child because of rising waters.

"Why *Dolomedes dondalei?*" asked the Stone Wētā.

The girl who might be the Fish-eating Spider shrugged. "There aren't many species where individuals go hunting for prey bigger than they are," she said. "I found it refreshing."

"You're angry."

"My home is being swallowed up by climate. No one gives a shit. You think my family was the last to leave? Hell, we weren't even the first. We left years ago. I can't even speak the language anymore! How's that for transformation?

"No one gives a shit," she said again. "It's all screwing with data now, trying to pretend that nothing's happening. Fine. We're all going to pretend everything's *fine*. I can pretend too. But I'm going to pretend with an insect I can at least admire for gumption, because God knows the people around me don't have any."

"It's a dangerous identification though, isn't it?" said the Stone Wētā, remembering the sound of ancient trees gone quiet, of the silence where Bristlecone Pine had been. She couldn't let anyone else get involved without making sure that they knew the risks they were taking. "Identification like that might make it easy to forget that hunting generally goes the other way."

The girl narrowed her eyes, and for an instant the Stone Wētā could see in them the shadow of many legs. "Sometimes danger is necessary," she said.

Dendrocnide moroides

The gympie gympie covers itself with stinging hairs and neurotoxin. It is one of the most poisonous plants in the world, and one of the most painful. A human who brushes up against a gympie gympie will experience agony for up to two years: it is a most persistent reminder of trespass.

It flourishes best after disturbance, when the ground is overturned and in full sunlight.

The Gympie Gympie buried her caches in shallow soil. She didn't use a single lockbox, didn't add to the same location more than once. Instead there were a dozen little burials, all in the open air with gaps in the rainforest canopy above. Atop each burial she planted a small specimen of *D. moroides*.

She wore protective gear when she planted; amused herself by picturing what would happen if some poor bastard came looking for what he shouldn't. The Gympie Gympie's ancestors had walked the tropical ecosystems of northern Australia for tens of thousands of years before the Europeans came, and she had been raised with their knowledge, had gone away to university for ecology and come home to her own lands.

She didn't much care if she were followed; there were more dangers here than interrogation, than imprisonment and the betrayal of science. No one that followed would know those dangers like she did. Anyone alien enough, who didn't know what they were getting into, deserved what they got as far as the Gympie Gympie was concerned. There was a reason she supplemented the buried seeds of science with silica and poison, and it was so the lands of her childhood weren't ravaged further than they had to be when the climate turned.

The Sand Cat might have prioritized preservation, but the Gympie Gympie was all about justice. Her own country wasn't so fucking innocent, and she had no pity left in her burials for guilt.

❋

Buellia frigida

This Antarctic lichen of the Dry Valleys grows slowly, perhaps a single centimeter for every millennia, but it does grow. The lichen is so accustomed to extreme cold and aridity that it is used as an approximation of what life may be capable of on Mars. Experiments on the International Space Station, where the lichen is exposed to the conditions of space, as well as to a simulation of Martian environments, prove that the lichen is capable of enduring both.

✵

The Antarctic Lichen floated through the ISS, making her way to the docking port. The transports to the Mars colony were almost ready to go, and the scientists that had been ferried up and through the ISS to their respective ships had almost been offloaded. Only a few were left, and the Antarctic Lichen, assigned on permanent rotation to the Station, was going to say goodbye.

She didn't know the Stone Wētā, had never been informed of her true name, but when the Stone Wētā had first stepped aboard with the tattoo curling round her forearm, all spiky legs and long antennae and big striped body, the Antarctic Lichen had recognized her.

"Nice ink," she said.

"Kind of a last minute reminder," said the Stone Wētā, smirking. "I'm still not entirely sure of what. Endurance, maybe."

"Persistence," said the Antarctic Lichen. "Rebirth, into a different world." The world below them hung in space, green and blue and with the ice at its edges draining, the polar caps melting away almost as she watched.

"Transformation," said the Stone Wētā. "I am … familiar with the concept."

There was little chance to talk. But as the Stone Wētā prepared to disembark, the Antarctic Lichen gave her a small box. "If you could transport that over to your ship I'd be grateful," she said. "Last minute additions for *Buellia*. Just pass them on, please."

Anyone around them would have thought the box was to be handed over to the colony's botanical department. *B. frigida* was making the trip, after all, and it gave the Antarctic Lichen some comfort to know, after all her experiments on it, that if the lichen's native environment was at risk then there was, still, the potential for it to survive on other worlds.

Mars had the potential to preserve a lot.

"It's amazing what can survive in such inhospitable places," said the Stone Wētā.

"I have every faith," said the Antarctic Lichen, waving through the window in the airlock. It was perhaps paranoia that made her send data to the open plains of another planet, but she couldn't keep hoarding on the ISS, where there were limited opportunities to unload.

Data that couldn't be shared was always at risk.

The Fish-eating Spider stared up into the dark. Though she could not see it, the ship carrying the Stone Wētā had begun its journey to a harder planet. The Fish-eating Spider did not envy her. She would have missed the stream-sides, the night-sounds of water and the creatures that lived beside it. The way the earth smelled when she turned it over for burial, the shovel new-bought and shiny in her pack.

A drive of smuggled data hung between her breasts, waiting for the morning.

Come Water, Be One of Us

In March 2017, the New Zealand Parliament passed a bill recognizing the Whanganui River as a person. Days later, India accorded similar recognition to the Ganges and Yamuna Rivers. In May 2017, the same recognition was given to Rio Atrato in Colombia.

It was a mistake recognizing corporations as people. They weren't, not really, but it was a convenient fiction and we've always been good at those.

We never saw where it would lead.

Try convincing a corporation it isn't a person now, see how far it gets you. There's whining and litigation and they slouch down the street after you, cat-calling. "Look at me, bitch! I'm talking to you!" The sticky, greedy hands, the look of fake innocence they give when caught trying to shove those hands into your back pocket. Whether they're groping for arse or wallet doesn't matter, the response is always the same. "Teach me to be better! I can learn if you take trouble with me. It's your own fault I'm so unsocialized. You've got a responsibility to me."

But no one wanted that responsibility. We'd all gone sick on that after making them people in the first place. Corporations were never meant to be people. As people, they are total fucking failures.

Some of them are vicious. Some of them are really bloody thick.

All of them are out for themselves.
All of them drown.

We made the corporations people, but then we did the same to the rivers.

It was a way of fighting back. It was the best thing we ever did.

Oh, some people didn't think that way at first. I don't know what they expected — like somehow the Whanganui would rise up, burst its banks and drag down to a watery grave every person who ever tossed their beer cans into it, every kid who ever pissed themselves while swimming. No, that's a lie. I do know what they expected, and those expectations were all to do with gain.

"If it's a person, is it going to pay taxes now?"

"If it's a person, can we lodge a claim against it for flooding?"

Stupid questions, serious questions, because a river might have arteries and waste products and it might be the beating heart of a people, even, but a person, we think, should have *personality,* and there's more to that than the way they look after storms, or the color they turn in sunlight. Personality has quirk and vengeance and responsibility, the ability to choose. The ability to walk away.

If a river is a person, it could walk away.

If it's a person, well… how badly can you treat a person before they decide they just don't have to take it anymore?

How many beer cans, how many outlets? How much can we take and take and take, before we teach the river what taking's like, and how easy it is to do?

There's so much the water can take back.

Look at the corporations, greedy bloody things, gorging on the streets as they are. The rest of us pay tax, you'd think if some people paid tax then all of us would, but it turns out that if the characteristics of your personhood are big and business, you get to skate on by certain aspects of civic responsibility. They're happy to stand out then, their hands held out for special exemption, because if your profit margin's big enough, you can ignore the fact that all your employees are on welfare, needing more than slim wages and poor working conditions to make ends meet.

Perhaps it's greed that makes a person. *I want, I want…* and all that wanting has gravity, it adheres to itself, forms a great sticky mass, and what comes out can pass for people. And suddenly there's this poppet walking around, person-shaped but with insides that are concerned with nothing but gold and greenbacks and reproduction, because every living thing has the potential to reproduce itself and when there's nothing else in there but greed, everything other than the urge for *more* is blunted. It's clutching for cash all the way, for influence and the power to ruin others.

I think they get off on it.

Expect different — demand different — and get crushed. And after, get gone, because even if corporations are people then they're canny ones, and you can only put the people those fuckers hire into the dock, not the corporations themselves. Personhood only goes so far and there's only henchmen left, the ones so hollowed out by their own bulging *want* there's nothing left inside them but empty space for corporations to nest in.

If this were the middle ages, we'd drown those lackeys for witches, to be so possessed by another. Perhaps that's why we turned to the rivers, because there's one thing more essential to life than money and that's the end of thirsting. The richest person in the world can't live for more than three days without water. No surprise, then, that when the time came to push the corporations back we did it by hiding behind water.

The rivers aren't a ducking stool, but they'll do for all that. There are always people in need of drowning. It doesn't matter if they're people by biology or law, so long as they can't stop stuffing themselves, gorging on fear or attention or ego until their lungs give out.

Water is our witchfinder now.

It all comes into easy focus when the rivers pull themselves up over banks. There's a sort of slouching, heavy movement to it at first, nothing liquid like you'd expect because they're trying to hold all that liquid in, to give themselves shape and stop slopping around, because when we made them people, we gave them all the things we think of people and that included form.

They're not very good at it. The corporations are better — not perfect, but better — because they need to pass as best they can. Assimilation makes it easier for them to feed. The rivers care less about passing, because they can feed regardless.

Even before seeing them, you can tell. All that weight of water in footsteps behind, and they're not anything that anyone wants to toss a can at then, because there's the risk of a fist forced down your throat and drowning on it.

I saw it happen, once.

I don't know what he did. Pollution, corruption, exploitation. It must have been something, to provoke such a response. The river used to rise up sometimes before it became a person, too; it broke its banks and drowned people around it, and there was never a reason then. Yes, water cycles and heavy rains, I know, but I'm talking about *motivation*. Before the river was a person, it didn't have a will. It just *was*.

Maybe giving it personhood gave it motivation. It could have been nothing, could have been rain in the mountains, but the way the river surged towards that poor bastard, dragged him inside itself and under with such force that even through meniscus I could see the dislocation of the limbs, the way it filled him up, tore him apart... there's something *personal* in that kind of violence.

When the river walked away, after it had spat out most of what it had pulled under, that spat-out substance was just desiccated, dried-up, with all the liquid sucked out. What was left was pulverized, and blew away in the wind.

The part of me that had frozen while watching, unwilling to draw attention, expected the water to have pinkened, somehow, taken on if for only a moment the color and patina of flesh.

Nothing. Such a small amount of blood, of cellular fluid. A few liters only. It couldn't possibly make a difference against the weight of all that water.

The river walked past me when it was done, didn't even turn its head. As if I were no more than a mosquito, too unimportant to make even a dent in its resting surface. There's an advantage to being small.

I kept quiet until it passed. I did not look at the dusty remains of meat while water could possibly see me watching. I kept my eyes averted until the river shambled around the corner, until I could no longer feel the slosh and reverberation of its footsteps.

Then I ran away, still not looking.

People protect themselves, when they can. If they have the means.

He must have deserved it, meat or poppet that he was.

He must have deserved it.

When we made the corporations people, we made them like us. We taught them *want*, we taught them privilege and power.

When we made the rivers people, all we had left to teach was self-preservation.

You all know who I'm talking about. You've all met them. You've all *seen* them.

They're the ones who hike up drug prices because desperate people will pay to live, if they can, at the price of food and heat. They're the ones who get sent to jail for bilking shareholders but not for killing the poor, because a person hollowed out by a corporation is something more deserving than human, and to the corporation, all other citizens are cattle. Not providing vet care isn't a crime — not a serious one, at least.

They're the ones who pour poison into the environment, because it's cheaper to pollute than to dispose of it properly. And they don't live where they shit, so it doesn't matter what's destroyed as long as it's out of sight, and the effects are only suffered by other people.

They're the ones who lie about the climate, the ones who use child labor, the ones who undermine worker's rights and mismanage resources and buy their way out of legislation that might put a leash on what they're able to do.

"Everyone would do it if they could," says a corporation, stirring sugar into its coffee as it's interviewed about the poor safety record of its international factories. "Exploitation is a human characteristic. You could almost say it's a human right."

Right.

I saw a mob once, chasing a man. Chasing something man-shaped, perhaps, but I'd felt those fingers in my back pocket, groping, so I chased him too. We dragged him down, beat him, threw him in the river. No one ever found the body.

"How could you?" said the other corporations, after. "He was a person, too."

"Yes," we said. "A person just like you."

They were all a little more careful around the river, after. A little more careful around the rest of us, too.

There's blood in our veins, but most of blood is water. Rivers run through our veins more than balance sheets ever did.

There's people at the river mouth now, every day. They come down with flowers, set them floating, bring their mouths down to the surface and drink.

The new communion. Some call it cannibalism, but I think the water's just calling home. We feel more like people, after.

The river seems so much more a person, after.

(A corporation seems so much more a poppet.)

Tomorrow we go to court again.

Tomorrow the forests will be people too.

Indicator Species

There were too many otters to name. Niall had named them as a child, the few he had managed to see; they were better than the friends he didn't have at the school he didn't go to, and the home he didn't want to go back to. As a young man he'd forgotten the names he had given them, and the river was a place of temptation and absence, somewhere he'd had to be fished out of when it all got too much, and for many years after that he'd avoided it. Careful in his footsteps, careful in his medication, and the latter helped but the former didn't. He was too cut off, spent too much time looking down as if concrete and pavestones would make sense of his life, would map some sort of route out of depression and into health.

The first time he went to sit by the river, after, he remembered the taste of river water in his mouth. A muddy taste, and not unpleasant. Thinner than he might have thought. The river bank was bare, mostly, and the water was brown, mostly, and he sat and watched and hoped for movement because that would mean he was watching something other than the memories of himself.

Across the river, he remembered, had been a holt, and it was the first experience of river that didn't involve shame that he could recall. There had been a holt and a slide, and an otter, once, in a city where he had not thought to see otters, or not many of them.

He watched and there was nothing, and he walked and there was nothing, just the vertical stretch of city up above him, and he might have called it looming if it weren't so indifferent to life. It took him a week of walking to remember that otters were more active at night and another week to find one, a small sleek presence hanging on in a place inhospitable to it, and Niall felt an admiration for it, a small, yearning seed of kinship.

Mental health, so he had been told — by pamphlets and doctors and counselors, by academic reading and the distant, hurtful recollections of childhood — improved with access to nature.

Perhaps by helping the otters he could help himself. Perhaps it was possible for them to be so connected, instead of isolated creatures wary of crowds and of being seen.

Otters, glossy, sinuous predators, could only thrive in numbers if the food web beneath them was stable, and well-filled. They were an indicator species: a measure of health and riparian life. There had been so few of them when Niall was a child. He'd wandered the banks of the river, of all the city's rivers, and he'd pretended there were more otters than there were, because if there were more otters then there was more everything, and he lived in a better world than he did, one greener and more hopeful.

Water, he thought, should be more than a reminder of emptiness and a temptation to drown. It should be a place of planting, because if the riverbanks were leafy, pleasant places they were stability, too, and bulwarks against erosion. It should be a place of clarity, because water when clear enough could be seen through, seen ahead, and obstacles more easily navigated. It should be a home for the creatures that lived in and beside it, who came to drink there and feed there and play there, because then it was a welcome rather than a reason to turn away.

He'd started with the planting, on his own, in an out of the way corner that was mostly rubbish and broken bottles, an ugly place for a man who felt ugliness all the way through him. He didn't ask permission. He didn't think he should have to, and besides, he was afraid of other people, and of their judgment.

Looking back, he thinks he shouldn't have been. They were strangers who came to help him, at first. Half an hour here, a borrowed tool there, and it occurred to him that he was not the only one who felt cut off inside, who felt small and ugly and alone, and who wanted to live in a place full of life so that they could feel connected to that life. And then there were more people, and more, and more plants and more insects and more fish, more birds. More otters. Over the years, so many of them, and the people who had worked on the river went away, some of them, to work on city walls and city streets and little city corners of concrete misery and pigeons, because pigeons were all that could survive there, and they made the city a greener place, a river place, full of parks and wetlands and so many otters Niall could hardly name them all.

It didn't cure him. He still took his medication, still had appointments with counselors and health workers. His illness persisted ... but it wasn't all of him, and it was less than before.

You're Not the Only One

Marcus was meant to be going to the moon today. Years of training, years of anticipation. I can't imagine the letdown. Instead he's in the community garden, as usual, weeding. Marcus *hates* weeding. He'd rather prune the fruit trees or tie up the bean plants or be in the kitchen, cooking. Anything but weeds. "I'd like to say I feel a sympathy," he says, when I bring him over a glass of water. "That I know what it's like to feel out of place, and that's why I hate digging them up. But I picture myself saying that aloud and meaning it and it just sounds so bloody *whiny*. Can you get secondhand embarrassment for what future-you might have said?"

"Only if present-you has the common sense to recognize self-pity when he sees it," I say. I don't bother to say that weeds are good for compost. We both know it already, and besides, if anyone deserves to have a few moments of private self-pity today it's him. "Shit day. I'm sorry."

"Hey," he says, stretching out his back, and even having been hunched over for the past couple of hours he's more graceful than I am. I'd get down on my knees to help him finish the last of the rhubarb patch, but when I'm this pregnant it'd take a winch to get me back up again. "It's not over, it's just put off for a bit. There are a lot worse things."

He doesn't look at my belly as he says it, not even a passing glance, so I know that he's not thinking of me. And because he's a kind man, even in the midst of his own terrible disappointment, he winces when he realizes what he's just said. "I didn't mean Hannah," he says, and it was the right decision to give her a name, even if she'll never take more than a few breaths with one. "Is it better or worse to say I wasn't thinking about her at all?"

"Horribly, I think it might be an improvement." It's not that I don't appreciate the sympathy, but it all gets a little cloying sometimes. I miss being treated like a person, instead of a vessel of tragedy. People try, of course they do. But sometimes pity, for a future gone wrong, or gone unexpected, is hard to take. "But if it makes you feel better, yeah, there's part of me a little glad not to be the only one to experience crushing disappointment this year. Oh, and you missed a spot."

Marcus glares at the weed, and laughs at me. "I see how it is. No coddling required. Well then, get your massive self down here, if you can, and help me weed the rest. I suppose I can heave you up afterwards."

"I'm not that big," I huff at him, but that's an absolute lie. I feel like an elephant. Elephants are pregnant for over eighteen months, so Marcus is right: it could always be worse. I don't think I could stand being pregnant for eighteen months, not when I know that Hannah won't live long past her birth. I guess in that respect the elephants are lucky: they don't know when disaster's coming for them.

Then again, neither do we. Melting ice at the poles has released more carbon dioxide than expected — much more, and it's blown the global carbon budget. That's why Marcus is grounded right now. Space exploration is a wonderful thing, but it's environmentally expensive and we need to balance our priorities.

"I should have expected it," he says. "I've seen the numbers. I guess I let hope get in the way. Well, not hope. Wanting. I don't think they're the same."

"Only sometimes." I'd hoped for, and wanted, a healthy child, but scans showed that Hannah had abnormalities that were incompatible with life. I had no hope for her, but I still wanted her ... even if I only had her for a little while. It helped to know that she wouldn't be in pain, and that some of her organs would help other children who had a little more hope to go with their parents' wanting. "There's different kinds of hope. I don't think wanting things for ourselves is any less bad than wanting things for everyone. You've just got to find a balance you can live with."

"Hence the weeding," says Marcus, clearing another space around the rhubarb plants. "I thought I could sulk at home today, feel sorry for myself, or I could come do something useful."

"You don't even *like* rhubarb." There's a lawyer who works in the kitchen garden sometimes who loves the stuff, and is always bringing in rhubarb muffins. They taste pretty good, but I've never seen Marcus choke one down, not even to be polite.

"Can't stand it," he says cheerfully. "It's revolting. But I got here early and I saw the bed needed a weed and I had to laugh. No trip to space, and now *rhubarb*. The universe is clearly out to get me."

"Suit yourself. I mostly came for the strawberries." They're planted besides the rhubarbs, a small field of them, and I'd like to say it's Hannah who's responsible for just how many of them I've managed to eat, but I've loved them ever since I was a kid myself, so it's only fair that I do my share of looking after them. I'm not the only one who likes them, either. "No strawberries on the moon," I say, nudging him and nearly overbalancing with it.

"No rhubarb either," says Marcus. "Damn, but I wish I were there."

"I know. Are you coming tonight?"

"Don't really feel much like celebrating, to be honest."

"It's not a celebration, it's a pity party. For us, not you. We thought we were shot of you; turns out we've got you for a bit longer anyway. Come along and rub our noses in it, why don't you."

"You're a cruel and heartless woman. Go on then. I accept."

The entire neighborhood was at the party. A mutual decision, to make it a celebration anyway. No one's quite sure for what, but why be miserable when you don't have to be? It's an exercise in compassion, I suppose. We all know how disappointed he is; the thought of one of us going to the moon to build a base there, the first of the colonists ... it's a childhood dream, and we got to be a part of it by proxy.

Childhood dreams rarely involve "Not now, but later."

Maybe that's what we're celebrating. That we've come together enough for there to be a later, that we've collectively developed the compassion not to let dreams get in the way of decency. That we have, as a society, decided to be adults. What use is it to go to the moon if the tides that moon influences are so very much larger than before, that they drown the coastlines beneath us, that they send entire nations into homelessness and want?

It may be an exhibition of smugness to celebrate selflessness, but the celebration is an indication of value. Marcus knows it too. I can see his shoulders relax as the night goes on, see his gestures become more open, hear the laughter without a tinge, at last, of bitterness. Part of that could be the booze. Last year's cider has come in, the orchard next to the school well-tended. There's beer brewed from the hops grown on the roof of the community center, and of course everyone has a lemon tree. We can't sweeten lemonade with sugar anymore because it doesn't grow here, but there are beehives in the garden and we get honey enough to substitute.

"I'm going to try making limoncello," Marcus says to me. He's brought over a plate because I've had enough of standing for a bit, too much weight on my feet. "Jamie's been experimenting with the potatoes again, says she's got a good vodka going. I reckon if I can set up an air circulation system so far above the Earth I can manage a still now."

Jamie and I share glances across the room and try not to laugh. Marcus has tried stills before. It never goes well. I remember a cucumber gin that was brown and tasted nothing like cucumbers. Marcus had drunk it anyway, trying not to wince. "It'll toughen the stomach," he said, but none of the rest of us were game. I mean really, wastefulness is a ridiculous thing but there are limits. He's not managed anything drinkable yet, but this party is to celebrate postponement as much as anything else: the idea that anything can be achieved with dedication and time, that a dream deferred isn't a dream given up on.

"Have they set a date yet?" I ask him.

Marcus shrugs. "For the next launch? No. It'll be a couple of years at least, I think, depending on how much carbon we can claw back." He smiles as he says it, and it's bittersweet. The local school kids had offered, earlier, to forego their yearly camp, wanting to contribute their share of carbon reduction so that he could go to space just a little earlier. The emissions from their transport might be small, but every bit added up. He hadn't accepted, though we'd all seen how touched he'd been, and the kids had bargained down to some extra days of planting. The lawyer who made the muffins that Marcus so loathed — there had been muffins tonight, brought as contribution to the meal and as usual demolished by everyone but him — had a son who specialized in wetlands, and who was organizing to restore a small stream. The kids could help with that, both with planting and restocking the stream with eels and fish, and in return Marcus would visit the school and talk to them about disappointment, how to live with it and turn it into something better, and how it wasn't the end of dreams.

"What about you?" he says. "Set a date yet?" It's a difficult question, and one I wouldn't have brought up on my own, not at a celebration that isn't about me. For Hannah's life to have the most impact, for her to be able to make her own great contribution, the birth would have to be carefully managed. Induction was set for only a few weeks away. Part of me couldn't wait to meet her, and the other part wished to keep her with me forever, elephantine pregnancy or not.

"Yes," I say, "but I'd rather not talk about it right now if that's alright. It's supposed to be a happy day."

"It's supposed to be but it's not," he says. "Don't look like that, I'm doing my best. I'm grateful for what I've got, for the opportunities I've had. But it's not the same."

"No. It isn't."

"Well," he says. "In a minute or two I'm going to ask you to dance, if you think you can manage it. We'll spin about a bit and pretend to be happy until we are. It probably won't take that much. But before then, if you can spare an hour or so in the next few days, Matt would like to talk to you."

Matt was his brother, an artist who I spoke to rarely these days because he preferred to spend his time in the garden tending to the greenhouses, and the humidity there made me uncomfortable now.

"Sure thing. I haven't had much of a chance to talk to him tonight anyway."

"Great. Up we go then. Jesus. Are you sure you haven't expanded since this morning?"

"You bastard! I have not. I think."

"Well, don't expect me to dip you or anything. I don't think my back could take it."

"Pity your feet can't," I say, tartly, and contrive to step on them at every second spin. It makes the both of us laugh, but me a little bit more.

Marcus isn't the only one to visit the school and speak of disappointment. Honestly, I thought twice about it. Changed my mind more than once, but there's a responsibility, isn't there, and you can't argue for the value of compassion without being willing to receive the same. The kids might be young, but they deserve the dignity of being allowed to be kind.

I went the week before Hannah was induced. That way they could feel her even if they couldn't see her, though of course I took along the ultrasound photos so they could see her face while she was still alive. I don't know how many of them have seen an adult cry before. I hope I'm not the first. The questions are different to the ones I'm used to.

"Are you going to have a birthday party?"

That one hurts.

"Hannah isn't going to live long enough to have a birthday party," I tell them.

This strikes them all as monstrously unfair. I didn't think I'd find myself laughing, but the absolute indignation on their faces is horribly funny. The conversation devolves into the kind of birthday cake that Hannah would like best, if she were able to live long enough for a birthday and solid food. I tell them how much I like strawberries and that's the decision-maker: a sponge cake stuffed with strawberries and cream.

I'm not sure I'll ever eat one again. It's not their fault; they're doing the best they can. And it's not like I'm here for emotional support. That would be unfair to expect. They're only kids, that shouldn't be on them. It's important that they learn to feel for other people, to be comfortable with their emotions, but some things are as yet beyond them.

One of the kids asks about termination. She's twelve years old, and that's not a discussion I was expecting to have but I've always thought anyone old enough to ask a question should have it answered honestly. "I thought about it," I tell them. "I wondered if it would be kinder to let her go quietly, to let her go to sleep before she was old enough to be born. And I wondered if it would be kinder to me, if it would hurt less that way. I didn't know what to choose. I didn't think either choice was bad, and kind people would have helped me either way. But in the end I decided that making it hurt less was maybe not so important. The only way to be hurt this badly when someone dies is to love them, and it's not good to live without loving someone. Grief isn't a bad thing. You're all going to feel it one day, if you haven't already, and it's important to be kind to yourself when you're sad, and to let people be kind to you, and to be kind to them when they are grieving too."

It was something I tried to remember when Hannah was born and the school sent a packet of cards and drawings. I opened the first one and it said "Welcome Hannah! I'm glad you're here and I'm sorry you don't get to stay" and when I stopped bawling I gave myself permission to pack up the rest and read them later, when her absence was an accomplished thing. (When that *later* came, months afterwards, it was ... I don't want to say it was a relief to read them, because relief isn't quite the word, but I was glad to see her acknowledged, her existence celebrated, because she deserved it and so did I.)

Before Hannah passed, the nurses at the hospital made ink prints of her little hands, her little feet. I took them with me when I went back to the school to tell the story of what had happened to her. I told them about the child who had received her corneas, and how he would grow to see the world through a lens of generosity. I told them about the child who received her heart, and how he would grow to feel kindness pulsing through the world like a living thing. I told them about the child who received her lungs, and how she would breathe in the air of a world where all the living creatures were connected.

The kids asked if the grief was worth it.

I told them that it was.

"I knew that Hannah might be able to help other people grieve a little less, perhaps, and that seemed like a good thing. I think if she were healthy, I would like to see her grow into a child as kind and clever as all of you. A kid who would help people if she could. I wanted to give her the chance to make a difference."

I got home, feeling wrung out, and found a couple of bottles of limoncello left on my doorstep, from a man who had visited the same school not so long ago to speak of his own disappointment, who knew how it felt to flay yourself open before others and to stand upright, still, and accept instead of scream. I drank myself silly and sobbed into pillows until they were as covered with snot as I was, and I woke in the morning with a pounding headache and not much sense of relief.

Two days later I dropped back the empty bottles. "You look terrible," Marcus observed. "Want to come weed the strawberries with me?"

He'd taken over my own volunteer hours at the community gardens, I'd heard. Him and a few others, contributing what they could so that I'd been able to have the time and space to grieve. I knew some people who wanted to work through their own trauma, who'd wanted routine and labor and something to structure their days by, but that hadn't been me, and so my own needs had been quietly accommodated.

It had been a while since I'd been to the gardens. I found it hard to remember when. The past few months had done for all my sense of time.

"I can't promise it'll make you feel better," he says.

I go anyway and it doesn't, at first.

Marcus finds me in the memorial garden. It's not just for Hannah, though the sculpture his brother made to help me remember her is here, amidst all the other signs of remembering, for all the other grief and losses. The sculpture's a pretty thing. A little abstract for my tastes, perhaps, but there are times when I visit and see it out of the corner of my eye and the pieces seem to slot together and shimmer, somehow, and it looks like a shining bird about to take flight. Three years since she died, and the thought of her now makes me smile before anything else. I'm considering trying again. I think I'd like that. I think that Hannah would have liked being a sister.

I know why he's here. Awkward, his hands not quite relaxed enough, wanting to be the first to tell me and not knowing that a friend had broken the news this morning, after she heard it from someone she worked with at the university, on the quiet.

I smile at him, and it doesn't hurt. "Carbon's under control again," I say, and Marcus winces.

"You heard."

Exploration is important. Going to the moon is important, and people all over the world have been saving, so that there's a chance for others to go ahead. The space program's back on, the moon shot brought out of abeyance, albeit a year later than anticipated. Marcus' dream will be realized on Hannah's birthday.

"I can remember and be sad for me and still look ahead and be happy for you," I tell him. No one has been crass enough to tell me that life goes on but it does, and that has come to be a comfort. There is comfort, too, in reciprocity, and how, in the past, he had put his sadness aside in service of mine. It would be shameful to do less.

"I'd rather it were any other day, but it's not up to me," he says. "And I know that sounds like I'm making this about myself."

"But there's going to be a party," I say, because of course there is. Why wouldn't there be? It's something to be celebrated, that one of us is going to the moon. A member of our community, reaching for the stars. "You're not going to be here for this one."

"Fingers crossed," he says. He stands beside me, and we contemplate his brother's sculpture, the clean lines and intimations of it, the quiet beauty. "I won't be upset if I hear you don't go."

"Of course I'll go." As if there was any question. "Would you be upset if I brought a cake? I know you won't be there, but it's your party really."

The scent of strawberries wafts over the hedge, warm in sunlight. "Something with candles," he says. "I think that'd be lovely."

Metamorphosis

A classroom full of ten year olds is perhaps not the best place to go when dressed as a cockroach, but they have come to expect it; I've worn costumes to class before as a way to catch their interest. Personally, I hate cockroaches. I know it's unfounded prejudice but they revolt me. I prefer beetles. They're no cleaner, no more worthy, but for me cockroaches are like rats. There's an intrinsic flinching, the quick classification of *vermin.* Which makes them perfect for introducing Gregor Samsa to the kids, because they are nearly all revolted too. I don't blame them. He was my brother, and he revolted me.

That, I admit, makes me wonder. Where does the revulsion come from? If Gregor had turned into a ladybug, and if, over a century later, I'd entered this classroom dressed as a ladybug, there wouldn't be this level of shared disgust. Yet with *The Metamorphosis* disgust is the point. I make sure to squirm round the classroom when they're reading, drag my antennae along the top of desks. The kids squeal and groan and giggle; one even retches and that would be mild success if it weren't me who'd have to clean the mess up if they did puke, so I pull back a little, and remove the headpiece for a discussion on revulsion. I keep my own hidden as much as possible, because I am at least attempting to be a better girl than the one who suggested to her parents that we ditch Gregor before his hideous presence ruined us entirely.

"How many of you have ever gone to feed the ducks?" I say. "Did you notice how the water just rolls off their backs? That's pretty cool, right? Well cockroaches have a similar ability. Their exoskeleton has a waxy coating that makes it waterproof."

It's about the nicest thing I can say about them, and I hope it seeds some questions. It's going to have to, because insects are about to be a big part of school life. We're trying to attract as many as possible, hence my resurrection of disgusting brother Gregor. That means we need to discourage stomping.

✹

Those of us with green roofs, we got used to it first. Mine is all over plants, natives and grasses and flowers, and because half my house is set underground, the roof is more accessible than most. I spend a lot of time up there, and I planted to attract the birds. They're such pretty creatures, full of easy appeal: tūī and bellbirds and fantails. There's even a little pond for them to drink from, for them to bathe in. And the birds do come, and I like to see them, but increasingly, on my green roof, I found insects.

At first I justified their existence on the grounds that some of the birds would eat them. I did love the birds, more than I distrusted the insects anyway. Although *distrust* is perhaps not the word. Discomfort, perhaps? We spend so much time clearing our homes of them. Don't want flies, don't want ants, don't want those horrible cockroaches. (I traveled as far from home as I could, and there are still cockroaches.) They all have connotations of filth and alright, so I could probably stand to dust a little more often, but I'd prefer to keep actual infestation out of the house. Weevils in the flour bin? No thank you. There's a limit to how adventurous I'm prepared to be with my baking, and although I've tried biscuits with insects in them, there's a difference between insect flour and biting into stinkbug.

I suppose the beetles became my gateway bug, when my brother absolutely failed to be so. There's so many of them, and I just ... I like their shape, those hardened little wing cases. I like their colors, and how there are so many of them. The mānuka beetle is a bright metallic green; I think it is my favorite, and the mānuka trees beside the house brush against the roof. I captured some of them and took them to school in jam jars to show the kids. They watched as the beetles ate young mānuka leaves, and I had them raid the green paints and start drawing. The back wall of the classroom is covered, now, in scarab shapes and observations of their behavior.

Children's response to insects, I have read, is dependent on positive exposure — mine, as a child, was entirely negative. And since the school has been given a grant to build green roofs on top of its classrooms, their exposure will soon be critical.

The Tanguru chafer beetle is also a bright green, and fringed with little hairs. I have not seen it often on my roof; it is a beetle that prefers to live in forests, where its young are underground and eating tree roots. My roof cannot support a forest, but with more and more homes having green roofs, more and more gardens are above, and the space between dwellings, once dedicated to the wasteland of lawn, is filled with trees. When I see a Tanguru chafer on my roof, it's because it has flown astray, perhaps, come a little out of its way and I like to think that it is on my roof because I have chosen to have a roof that, by proxy, brings forest back into the cities by allowing them space to grow.

I have a greater appreciation for nature than I did back when my brother was a cockroach. Time changes a lot but not everything; and if Gregor turned into an insect, I turned into a woman, but not an old one, not ever. The wonder of it has grown stale. These days I find my wonder in smaller forms.

The stag beetles are spotted and have curved mandibles. The tiger beetle is metallic bronze, with long legs. The pit weevil is one that I accommodate in the roof garden but rarely see. It lives in dead, decaying branches of native trees — I use beech, mostly, but take anything I can get — that I lug up onto the roof and leave in strategic spots. The pit weevil bores holes in the wood and lays eggs there. The four-spined weevil is a shiny, sculptural creature; it is my favorite after the mānuka beetle and I make sure that my roof garden has tree ferns alongside it, dropping dead fronds onto the roof where they provide easy access to food sources. The flower longhorn beetle is a dark almost-purple with yellow spots, the lemon tree borer has orange hairs around its eyes.

When I lie in bed at night, I think of the beetles above me, and how the roof has made a home for them when once roofs did no such thing. It saddens me to see bare rooflines now. Their houses seem sterile and empty, and I wonder at the selfishness that made us think houses should be homes for nothing but people. Perhaps if I'd be open to sharing when Gregor ... well. It does not do to look back.

There are many reasons to have a green roof. They insulate well, they counter air pollution. They are good for encouraging biodiversity, and they do bring the birds. For me, though, I have come to love them for the beetles, and then for the other insects. Butterflies, of course, everyone admires those — the orange monarch and the black and white magpie moth, for whom I keep a gorse bush in close bounds. The looper moth, the common blue, the white butterfly ... Then there are the mantises, which always seem to make their way inside, until I scoop them up and put them out again. Dragonflies, wētā, the passionvine hopper, they are all here. A bird is a pretty creature, but when I count a dozen different beetles on my roof in the evening, half a hundred other insects, I feel as if I am in an ecosystem, and not an impoverished one.

A home should be an ecosystem.

❁

I ask the kids why they're so revolted by cockroaches. To be fair, not all of them are, but some look at my costume with various iterations of illness on their faces. They're ugly, I'm told. They spread disease. They're filthy, and they *skitter*. Their mothers hate them. Their fathers hate them. If one finds its way inside the house there's sometimes even screaming. They are, the consensus is, *gross*. I agree with everything they say, though I do it quietly.

Who would write a story about cockroaches? they ask me. I tell them that the insect in *The Metamorphosis* was never named. When I told Franz Kafka what had happened to my family, I was very clear that Gregor turned into a cockroach. That did not make it through to the final version of the story. Franz didn't even want Gregor's insect self drawn on the cover of the book because it might give people an accurate identification. All he wanted them to know was that the insect was *monstrous*. It was *verminous*. He let people fill in the blanks themselves, and most people filled it with cockroach. (I could have told him they would have, but he always struck me as more optimistic than I was.)

I hand out art supplies and tell the kids I want them to make masks of the insects that revolt them most.

Some do choose cockroaches, because I'd put them in mind of cockroaches, but a couple come up to feel the suit, to see if it was as waxy as I claimed, and to stroke the antennae. More of the kids choose wasps or bees, because they sting, and honey doesn't make up for it they say. One girl makes a mask of worms. "I don't care if it's not an insect," she declares. "They squirm, and they're bald and meaty and *disgusting*."

It is the look on her face, that determined revulsion, that convinces me. It's like looking in a hundred year old mirror. I tell her to get on with it and make the best worm mask she can.

One child chooses cicadas, because even though she likes the little cases left when they split their skins and molt, their chirping annoys her. "There's heaps of them outside my bedroom window," she says. "They never shut up!" I have her move next to a boy who is making a mask of a field cricket. "Every night," he says. "On and on they go. I can't sleep with the racket they make!" But he has a plan. "There's a hedgehog in the garden. I can hear it crunching on the crickets. If anyone else has a hedgehog I'll swap you a packet of chips for it." "I wonder if they'd eat cicadas," says his new desk-mate, scowling.

There's even a kid with a grudge against a beetle — the striped lax beetle, which leaves blisters when touched. After an encounter with it on my roof, I can't say it's my favorite either, so I send him over to the Hymenoptera table, where they can all complain together. I hope none of them have a sibling that turns into a blister bug. That would be worse than what I got, I think.

At the end of the day, all the masks have dried and an entire classroom of insect faces stares back at me, along with one worm. One of the flies has sacrificed a tennis ball and cut it in half, gluing each side to his mask. He can't actually see out of it, but is clearly satisfied with his appearance.

Two dozen children with insect faces, and me in a cockroach suit. Gregor would be proud. Well, no. He probably would have wept. He always was too softhearted. If it had been me who turned into a cockroach, you can bet I wouldn't have starved myself for other people's convenience. I know he was my brother, but it wasn't *entirely* surprising he turned invertebrate. The boy simply lacked backbone.

"I hope you like your faces, kids," I tell them, "because next year, fingers crossed, all these things will be living here with you. Right up above us, in fact."

The insect children are distinctly — and severely — unimpressed.

"Gregor's sister Grete probably made that face," I say. (I had made that face.) "Maybe if she'd been less disgusted by him he wouldn't have starved to death."

Guilt. If you learn to feel it young it never goes away. "You don't want your insects to starve, do you?"

None of them are willing to say *yes*, but I can tell that some of them are thinking it.

Sometimes I wonder if it would have been kinder if I'd just smashed him, got him quickly from behind, instead of making him starve himself. It probably wouldn't have been kind either way.

(I don't tell the kids that last part. Guilt also makes for good role models.)

There are trees all around, where lawns used to be, for increasingly our leisure space is vertical. Lying on my roof garden is like lying in a meadow. An enclosed open space, full of grasses and flowers and small green things that do well in sunlight. It's where I go after I skin myself of the cockroach suit — goodbye, Gregor — and raise myself to a meadow that smells of mint more than other herbs, lavender and rosemary and basil. The walls below are green as well, trellised with vines around the windows although none of them span more than waist high because that's where the roof starts, the house extending down into earth. Above, solar panels sit between A-frames of beans and sweet peas, and tomato plants, and tussocks to store the rain water.

I've considered putting in a scarecrow, not that it would scare anything away. The birds already recognize a soft touch and the beetles wouldn't care. But this is a created space, a creative space, and scarecrows can be more than pouches of hay, the promise of strategy and intelligence. I think I'd like something sculptural up here, something more than the tussock leaves and weevils and pyramidal supports. There's room for more. Something light, I think, but solid. Something in pumice, maybe, because pumice is something I can never resist touching, and it can be carved into shapes, stacked and scattered and if it doesn't give the movement one might want from a scarecrow, I can always get a weather vane for that.

❋

The children are assigned projects on the least favored insects. They grumble a bit over it, but tough. Climate change has damaged biodiversity in this country, and that was before the ocean started rising, swallowing coastlines. They live in an archipelago, and there is no more tolerance for wasted space. Our gardens must be vertical now, our biodiversity preserved through roof tops and other exploitable spaces. We are making reefs of our cities, turning them into three dimensional surfaces to be colonized by organisms that are not us.

A diverse ecology is a strong ecology, and they will not be taught to pander to their own dislikes. I will not have them embarrassed by cockroaches ... because it is embarrassing to be so squeamish of them. There is no rational excuse. I can't say that I will ever love the creatures like I do the beetles, in the same way as I can't say that I ever truly loved Gregor, but love is not required for acceptance.

They'll learn about stings until they are no longer afraid of them. They'll build earthworm farms until they name the worms and take an interest in their welfare. They'll record cricket and cicada sounds, try to decode them and fail, and then try again. They will do this again and again, and I will make them, coax them, until the day that they can read *The Metamorphosis* and feel nothing but compassion for Gregor, and have revulsion be beyond them.

That's as much as I can do for him now, and more than I bothered with at the time.

Those children who live at homes that already have a roof garden are told to note down what insects they have, to make a journal of them. Those children who don't I invite to my own house, my own garden. I show them mānuka beetles and stag beetles, the flower longhorn, the four-spined weevil. They make lists of the beetles they would like to have in their own roof gardens, when grants come through to convert them, and on the roof gardens at the school, in the early stages of construction.

There is competition to bring insects from other homes, other roof gardens, to help colonize the new spaces.

By the end of the semester, the masks hang on a second wall, the wall not covered with drawings of scarab beetle, and everyone has begun to hate Grete. They don't know that she is me, of course — I changed my name long ago.

"Grete's a bitch," says one small child. The language is judgmental and a little inappropriate but I can't fault his conclusions. "He was her brother! It wasn't his fault he was gross. She should have spent more time trying to get used to him. They could have been friends if she'd tried harder."

"His parents sucked, too," says the girl at the next desk. "Just because he didn't look like everyone else doesn't mean he wasn't important too. They should have loved him better."

They should have. So should I. None of us did. He wasn't particularly lovable even before he became a cockroach, was Gregor, but we could have tried harder with him.

The cockroach suit has become familiar. It has worn out a little at the elbows. Exposure, it seems, is working, and not just for the children. I show the class videos of the giant hissing cockroaches from Madagascar, and they are all delighted.

I convince the school to buy some old fish tanks, and to use them as habitats. There aren't any Madagascan cockroaches to fill one of them, but we have a native variety. It will do. I still think the cockroaches are awful. A bit less awful than before, perhaps, and a bit more interesting, but then I have had more time than the children to settle into my prejudices and they are taking longer to pass away. It's a good thing I'm long lived.

One night, I dream that I am … not a cockroach, no. Reconciliation has not gone that far, not yet. I am not a mānuka beetle either. That's a shame. I would have liked to see myself in mirrors. All that lovely green. Instead, I'm something else. I don't quite know what; I've never seen one before. The next day I sit in my roof garden, the best part of my home — the home of so many creatures, now — and flick through field guides. It turns out I dreamed myself a flightless spiny longhorn beetle. It could never live in my garden. The plants are all wrong; I lack the dead trees necessary, and it seems a dead log would not do. Plus, they are rare in this country, and getting rarer. They need more habitat. They need people to love them enough to give it back, to consider their housing as much as our own.

The fish tanks line the third wall of the classroom. The fourth is reserved for future projects. The girl who hated worms is angling for a larger farm, so we can all see them tunnel through soil behind glass.

I'm going to tell them about the spiny longhorn. There must be something that can be done for it.

The beetle sculpture comes in pumice, and in parts. That last is deliberate. I don't want it connected up in a single piece; I can make a scarecrow of something else, perhaps. Instead, I scatter the beetle parts about the garden — a long antenna here, a wing cover there. Their curved parts peek at me from every corner of the garden, and they all provide shade and cover for the beetles that live beneath them. I think I like that better, and this way it means that, wherever I look, I can see a little beetle in the garden.

The image of cockroach is saved for the weather vane. Only a small one, but then again I don't need it to know which way the wind is blowing, and there are enough cockroaches in the roof garden anyway.

I make sure they have food.
 I am learning to welcome them.

The History of a Coral Future

This is a story of a reef. It's not a real reef. There are few fishes in it, and the corals are different. The reef is a metaphor.

When the future came, it was the only metaphor that mattered.

It started in orchards, rice fields, vineyards. Community gardens. Places for people to feed and come together. Places of gathering.

We used to think of ourselves as individuals first. A single organism of a single species, bound together with others of our kind, but that was never true. We never walked the world alone. If we had found a way to do so we would have died. Inside each seeming single body was a universe of other life: microbes, viruses, fungi. For each human cell, there were a hundred nonhuman ones; more of the DNA sheltered within us was alien than ours.

Each of us was multitude, our flesh and bones and blood a scaffold as coral was a scaffold in oceans. We were walking reefs, and our microbiomes were with us always. They were affected by where we lived, by what we ate, what we did … and they affected in turn. It was discovered that diversity within the microbiome, within the wondrous reef of us, was correlated with wisdom, and with loneliness. The more species we accommodated within us, the less lonely we felt. The less unwise.

In a world where the impacts of climate change came to rest so heavily on mental health, the microbiome protected us. All we had to do was feed it — and we fed it in the orchards, in the rice fields, in the vineyards and community gardens of our neighborhoods. Our suburbs were centered around food provision. Shared kitchens and shared work. Everyone was responsible. Everyone did their part. Surplus was offered to other communities — local communities. Bringing in food from far away standardized that food into transportable, often tasteless articles from a small number of species, and it meant excess carbon emissions and no grafting lessons in the orchards, no coming together to pick rice or press grapes, no one bringing their jugs to make cider together, no neighbors chatting to make weeding a more enjoyable task.

Our microbiomes needed each other. If diversity brought companionship and wisdom, them companionship and wisdom was thought, as well, to increase diversity within the microbiome. Our reefs were so lonely apart. We had to protect them, as they protected us, and that meant making sure no one was lonely again, that no one was left out or hungered for sustenance. Those who wanted time apart, who needed solitude more than others, could work early hours in the gardens, could work apart a little, and know as they did so that other people were always there to join when their microbiomes required it.

We plant for more than ourselves. There are trees planted that fruit only for birds, homes built for lizards and bats and insects, green corridors and clear water, woodlands and coastal grasses. In the in-between spaces we build memorials to what used to live there, and to what has survived there. Whale tails of stone erupt in parklands, schools of fish in bright metals woven into

orchards, great mechanical mammals placed on boulevards and brass arthropods studded along river banks, their heads polished where our hands have rested.

Our microbiomes whisper when we settle in shade beneath the giant ferns, constructed of driftwood washed ashore by rising waters. The earth beneath is damp, as it would be beneath the real ferns, which we visit often. "Are you lonely now?" they say. "Have you learned what we have told you?"

We lie back in that dark, moist soil and spread ourselves wide, arms stretched to encompass art and the earth it is planted in, all the microbes and the small, silent creatures of the world. We imagine the mites that live on our eyelashes, and wonder if we can mimic them in lanterns to light the paths at night, to remind us both that they exist, and that they are part of us, and lovely.

"Our eyelashes are close to coral," we tell each other, laughing.

✺

Then the reef came for the schools. A coral reef, that marvelous structure of shape and color, so vulnerable to climate, so difficult to restore, is characterized by biodiversity. A reef supports hundreds of species, thousands of them. Each one contributes to ecosystem, taking its place in a web of waves and wonder.

The schools didn't need to teach about ecosystems because the children were in the gardens, working with native organisms and introduced ones, working with seasons instead of against them, bringing worms and composts and birds, building roof gardens for insulation and pollution control, building green walls. It was a practical training. School time, equally practical, was for stories.

Languages and literature, until the age of adolescence. Mathematics was important, and history and science, but those were for older children, those who were well-developed in their empathy. Reef systems were built on community, on the importance of biodiversity in ecosystem, and the social ecosystem had, for too long, been too unbalanced.

Our stories were limited things, once. Opportunities for empathy, and we read what appealed, read characters that were like us, and too often only like us. Exposure to literature, to all sorts of literature, was proven to increase empathy, and schools for the youngest were stories, all stories, until our young were soaked in them, until superficial differences within the species were no longer barriers for consideration.

It was a failure of ours, for so long, that we could achieve competency in all subjects but this. It was a failure of character that some people were allowed to amass millions while those who did not look like them, who did not think like them, were allowed to starve, or to live without medical care, or to be shut out from opportunities that should have been their birthright. Failure, and disgrace.

When our children learn medical science, it is after they have learned to feel for the pain of others. When they learn of space travel, it is after they have learned to value the sustainability of home. They learn of vivisection after they have learned to love animals, economics after they have learned to love seeing others well provided for, mathematics after they have learned that other people count as well as they do.

Our children read and read and *grow*, because it is not guaranteed that they will meet enough people unlike themselves to learn to love those people as themselves, and exposure must come early or compassion never will.

Coral does not empathize, perhaps; but if companionship can support microbial diversity, then reef systems—strong in their variety and with webs of relationships embedded in ecosystem—can form sympathies that can characterize any community.

Sympathies and stories: they are the structures and the resolutions of laws that can beat back even the worst of greed, of ecological devastation.

✺

The schools, the libraries, have microbiomes of their own, have coral in the shape of shelves.

Our stories are painted over surfaces, on walls and floors and roads. They are wrapped around the trunks of trees, they are knitted into banners. The stories are painted, printed, embossed. We live in communities where verse is etched in Braille on streetlights, where window frames tell stories of metamorphosis and yearning.

We choose the stories we surround ourselves with. They are changed every year, so that none of us become too imprinted with familiarity, so that the steps we take through the streets and cities and byways of our homes become portals into fairy tales and romances and memoir. There is the story of a rising tide, there the story of migration, there again the loss of habitat. Stories of the stars, stories of the oceans. Stories of the people who explored them, and the people prevented from exploring them, and the people who chose to explore themselves instead.

There are the old stories, the ones that once were forbidden, that were no longer taught in schools because they were stories of a sundered people, kept from their culture and themselves. There are the new stories, where we learn to tell tales to illuminate our own lacks, and our capacity for taking, and the ways that we have found to loosen grip and allow what we have taken to be given back instead.

There are the stories of lands, the stories of lives.

There are the stories of reefs.

✺

Because our children are raised on the stories of others as well as themselves, they see the world in a multitude of ways. (There are so many eyes in a reef, so many ways of perception in a microbiome.) They no longer see the things that exist in that world through a single lens. And because our children are raised knowing that they are a multitude in themselves, their definition of self, and of personhood, is much broader than before.

They live in a world where personhood has become artifact. Centuries ago, when climate began to tear down the illusions that made us see the world as something beneath, rather than something beloved, a river was recognized as a person. It was legal protection, even if the people to whom the river *was* a person knew otherwise ... but that, too, was a relic of a time when Indigenous beliefs were also perceived as beneath. But then a river was a person, and another river, and another. Then a mountain, then a forest.

We made our landmarks people, and because we had come to understand people as reefs, as ecosystems, we made our ecosystems people too. A river was never just water; a mountain never just rocks and snow. They were systems as much as we were. So we made our landmarks people, and then we made ourselves — all of ourselves — believe it.

Stories and science, mixed together, and they made a legal system to change the world. To return it, perhaps, to what it had once been.

It is a healing thing, to visit with another ecosystem. We kept ourselves apart too long. All those new (old) people, all those old (new) ways of speaking. Algal blooms red upon the shore, blight in the forests, wetlands drying out. These are things to understand, and if you are taught to care for others, to ensure that their sickness is something that deserves healing, then you cannot draw back so easily when that sickness expresses itself in species loss, in ice sheet melt.

We had to claw them back.

We had to learn to atone. A mountain has no use for words. The forests swallow them whole, without tasting. The dead can't hear any apologies we might wish to give, and the ocean has always been too large to benefit from any salt our tears might give. Such things are fruitless. We had to learn when we were barren in our apologies, and we had to choose to do better.

When we are at the coast, singing in the spring tide, the one that surges higher than we like, the one that eats into land we would rather keep for ourselves ... that is the time for gratitude. For the ocean, too, is people, and it is not for one person to tell another where they can go, or what their nature is. The ocean may be wide and wild but it is living, too, and all its dead places are gone.

We are so careful, now, for life. A reef should be a lively place. We would be lonely if the sea were abandoned and empty. Our microbiomes would know the emptiness and cry out within us for ecosystem.

Treating it as a person has made our microbiome more diverse. It has made us a little more wise.

If only we'd realized, earlier, how much wisdom there is in reefs.

We invite the forests to festivals. There is so much to learn from them. They are rooted in place so the festivals must be held under branches, and we tell stories to the trees as we sing to the ocean, as we dance with the mountains. The stories come with small gifts — with rubbed glass taken from beaches, with little stones taken from mountains, with sculptures shaped from cities. When we go to those places in return, we will take old leaves to bury in sand, to scatter from heights, to press onto the sides of buildings and paint their shapes there.

The trees are linked themselves, roots systems and pheromones and it is taking us a long time to understand their language but we are trying, and trying, and one day their stories will be plainer to us. Their behavior changes when they are together — the chemistry and microbiology of intersection. Trees are social beings, they belong within a community. We wonder if any creature is ever really solitary. There are no more sad trees now, concreted into place and alone. If something has to be alone to stand out, to provide shade to a square or a fountain, it should be artificial instead of alive — a tree made out of libraries, of off-cut books and recycled timbers. Loneliness is no longer acceptable.

Their shared biology of root systems is so different from ours but "We recognize you," our microbiomes say, and we hear the wind in branches like the waves over reef.

Perhaps they recognize us back.

If a forest is a person, a forest can be a friend.

When we did realize, we began to make our own. It's not enough to be a reef, to learn to think like a reef, to include as reefs do. We wanted to live there as well.

Don't mistake us. There are no underwater cities, no submarine fancies come from rich men who were so deprived of stories not their own that they could never see further than themselves. That's not the kind of reef we care for, these days. We were living in reefs already, more of us every day, and it took us so long to realize it.

We called them *cities*. More and more of us urban dwellers, living in the midst of skyscrapers and overpasses, in three dimensional substrates that significantly increased surface area as the corals did. We didn't recognize them as corals at first — there's little wonder to find in the concrete skin of a car park building, or in ugly alleyways and sewer ways. We didn't realize they could be colonized by more than pigeons, more than rats. But then fish started colonizing underground storm systems, and the orchards and rice fields and vineyards and gardens came through from suburban systems to urban roofs, and we began to see possibility in the corners of architecture. So many ecological niches, and all of them able to be filled.

We filled them well. We deepened underground pipes, roughened their interior surfaces so that more fish, and larger, could swim more easily against currents. We took away cars and replaced them with fruit trees, we built wetlands around public libraries, because both were systems of resilience and stories made easy friends with swamps. We uncovered rivers. We built for birds as well as business, we turned every roof into a garden, every wall into a refuge. We built as if we were building coral, and we built for diversity, and for strength. When the climate changed it took so many species with it, and those it did not take were forced into environments that were less suitable for them, less able to be adapted to.

We were more capable of adapting than birds, more capable than fish and fungi and we had learned to value what was not ourselves, and we chose to adapt more quickly so that they wouldn't have to. The early schools, the community ecology of harvest, our books and our bodies ... these were training places for a broader urban ecology, for renewal and restoration, for learning to live with climate instead of insisting that it lived with us.

There is so much we had to learn tolerance for. There is so much that makes that learning worth it.

Reading. Eating. Naming. Making. These are things a reef can do. This is what it means, now, to be human.

✹

We were less human once. We burnt and boiled and choked, we let ourselves change the world instead of realizing that the world was inside us. We built cities that kept people out, that crammed them into boundaries based on accidents of biology, based on shades and degradations of greed. We kept our libraries confined, we limited our stories. We looked for reasons to misunderstand ourselves, and when we had cut our microbiomes down to nothing there was no wisdom that kept us from the rising seas, the changing climates. There was no compassion for the loss of homes and habitats. Slowly, surely, we were becoming a singular species, and we were killing ourselves to do it.

"You're destroying us all," said the microbiome, said the reef. "You diminish yourselves when you diminish us. We are so very sorry for you."

"We don't know what to do," we cried. "There's no changing this."

Can an ecosystem feel sorry for itself? Perhaps, if it's complex enough. Perhaps, if it's simple enough. We were complex creatures, and we made ourselves so very simple.

The capacity for change, they said, was in us already. We knew their names as we knew ourselves.

They showed us how to change, and so we did. We had to, because a reef is a marvel that should not be allowed to perish from this Earth, and that is true even when the reefs are us.

❋

This is the story of a reef.

This is the story of a billion of them.

They are all beautiful, and they are all real, and they are coming.

Story Credits

"We Feed the Bears of Fire and Ice" (2018) and "Come Water, Be One of Us" (2020) were first published in *Strange Horizons*. "The Stone Wētā" (2017) and "You're Not the Only One" (2022) were first published in *Clarkesworld*. "Gone to Earth" (2018) was first published in *Shimmer*. "Inside the Body of Relatives" (2019) and "Pollen and Salt" (2022) were first published in *Asimov's*. "Indicator Species" (2021) was first published in *Stories from 2050*. "Metamorphosis" (2021) was first published in *Triangulation: Habitats*. "Our Flesh Was Bred for This" (2019) was first published in *Frozen Wavelets*. "Resilience" (2020) was first published in *Stuff*. "The Body Politic" (2020) was first published in *Recognizing Fascism*. "The Streams Are Paved with Fish Traps" (2021) was first published in *Multispecies Cities*. "Tidemarks" (2021) was first published in *Professor Charlatan Bardot's Travel Anthology to the Most (Fictional) Haunted Buildings in the Weird, Wide World*. "Tranquillity" (2013) was first published in *Cosmos*.

About the Author

Octavia Cade is a speculative fiction writer from New Zealand. She has a PhD in science communication and a particular interest in how science is used in horror and science fiction that she likes to explore in both her academic and creative work. She has sold around seventy stories to various markets, and these stories increasingly focus on ecology and how people relate to their environment. Octavia attended Clarion West 2016. She was a visiting artist at Massey University in 2020 and the Ursula Bethell writer in residence at Canterbury University in 2023. She is currently plotting a non-fiction book on urban ecology.

YOU MAY ALSO LIKE

these titles by Octavia Cade and Tiffany Morris!

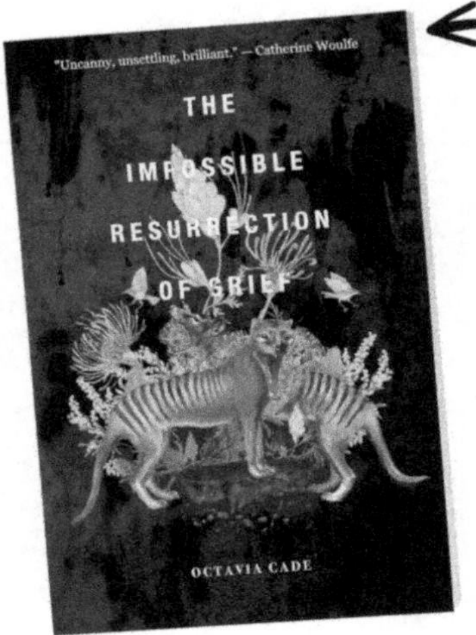

Resurrected thylacines and robot rock wrens populate this short novella about extinction and how we process grief.

In the dark rot of an east coast swamp, a queer Mi'kmaw artist is transformed by grief. A new novella by an emerging Indigenous author. Coming October 2023.

Earth-focused fiction. Stellar stories.
Stelliform.press.

Stelliform Press is shaping conversations about nature and our place within it. We invite you to join the conversation by leaving a comment or review on your favorite social media platform. Find us on the web at www.stelliform.press and on Twitter, Instagram and Facebook @StelliformPress and on Mastodon at mastodon.online/@StelliformPress.

Printed in the USA
CPSIA information can be obtained
at www.ICGtesting.com
LVHW010729290823
756540LV00009B/211